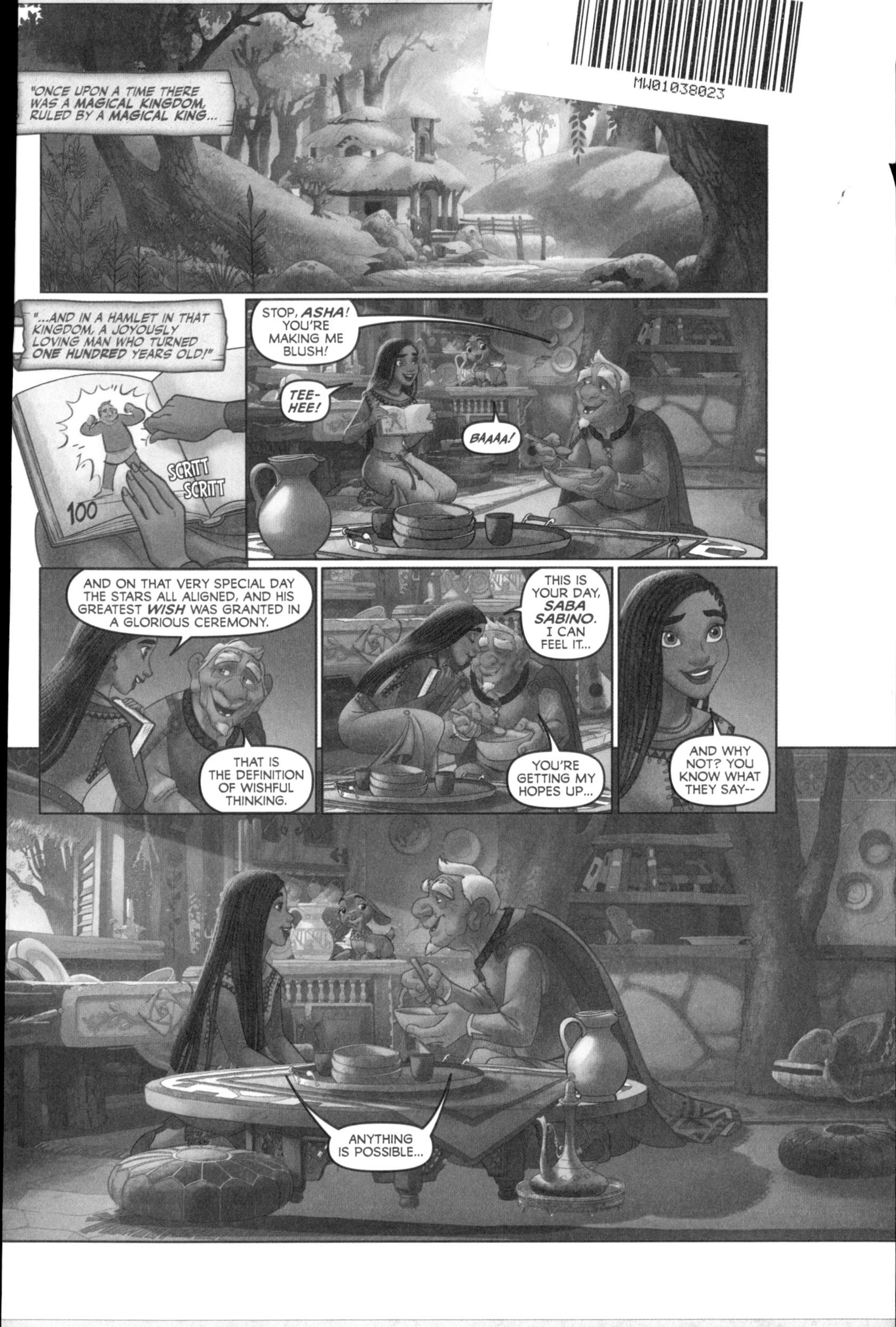
"ONCE UPON A TIME THERE WAS A MAGICAL KINGDOM, RULED BY A MAGICAL KING...
"...AND IN A HAMLET IN THAT KINGDOM, A JOYOUSLY LOVING MAN WHO TURNED ONE HUNDRED YEARS OLD!"
100
SCRITT SCRITT
STOP, ASHA! YOU'RE MAKING ME BLUSH!
TEE-HEE!
BAAAA!
AND ON THAT VERY SPECIAL DAY THE STARS ALL ALIGNED, AND HIS GREATEST WISH WAS GRANTED IN A GLORIOUS CEREMONY.
THAT IS THE DEFINITION OF WISHFUL THINKING.
THIS IS YOUR DAY, SABA SABINO. I CAN FEEL IT...
YOU'RE GETTING MY HOPES UP...
AND WHY NOT? YOU KNOW WHAT THEY SAY--
ANYTHING IS POSSIBLE...

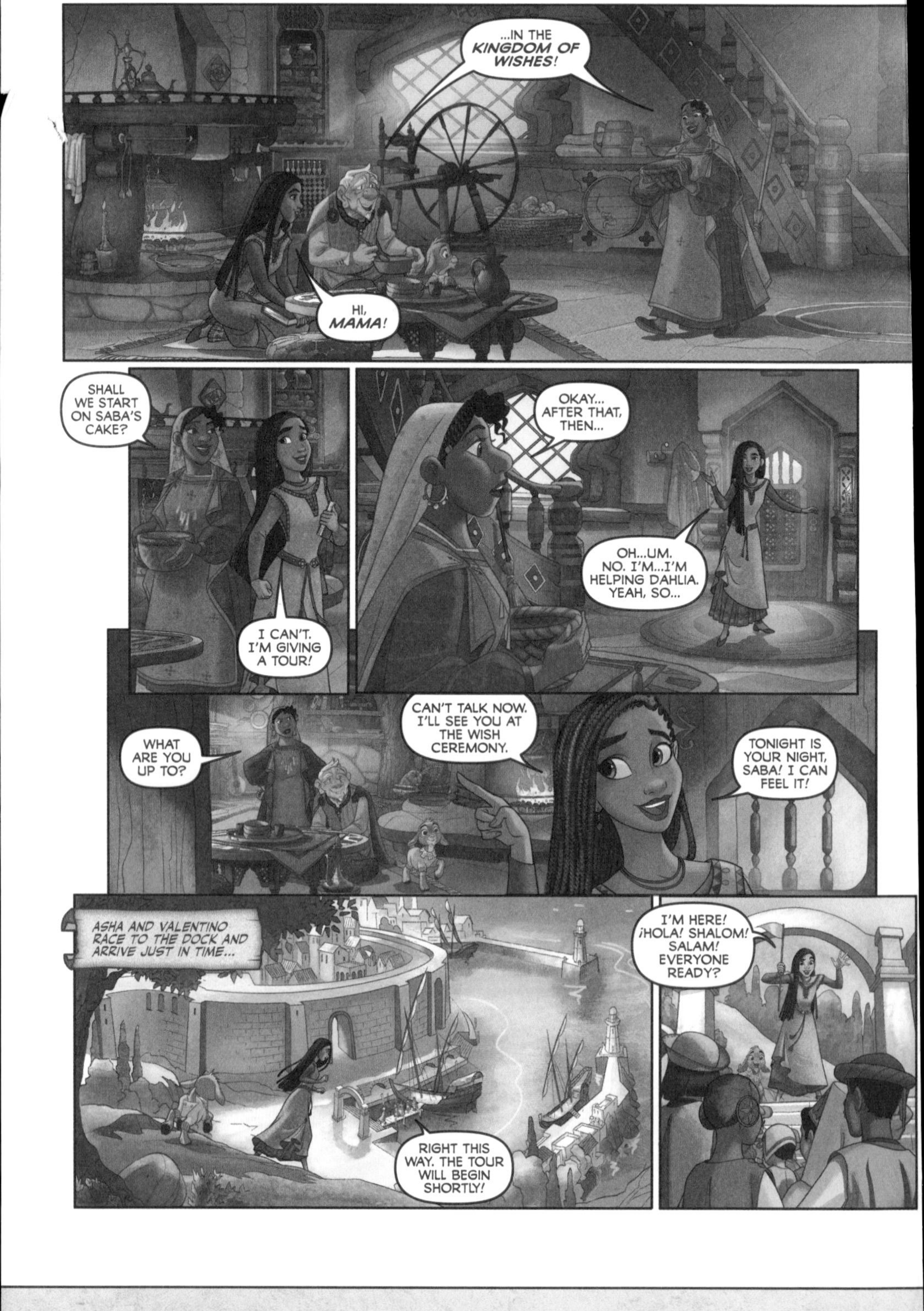
...IN THE KINGDOM OF WISHES!
HI, MAMA!
SHALL WE START ON SABA'S CAKE?
I CAN'T. I'M GIVING A TOUR!
OKAY... AFTER THAT, THEN...
OH...UM. NO. I'M...I'M HELPING DAHLIA. YEAH, SO...
WHAT ARE YOU UP TO?
CAN'T TALK NOW. I'LL SEE YOU AT THE WISH CEREMONY.
TONIGHT IS YOUR NIGHT, SABA! I CAN FEEL IT!
ASHA AND VALENTINO RACE TO THE DOCK AND ARRIVE JUST IN TIME...
RIGHT THIS WAY. THE TOUR WILL BEGIN SHORTLY!
I'M HERE! ¡HOLA! SHALOM! SALAM! EVERYONE READY?

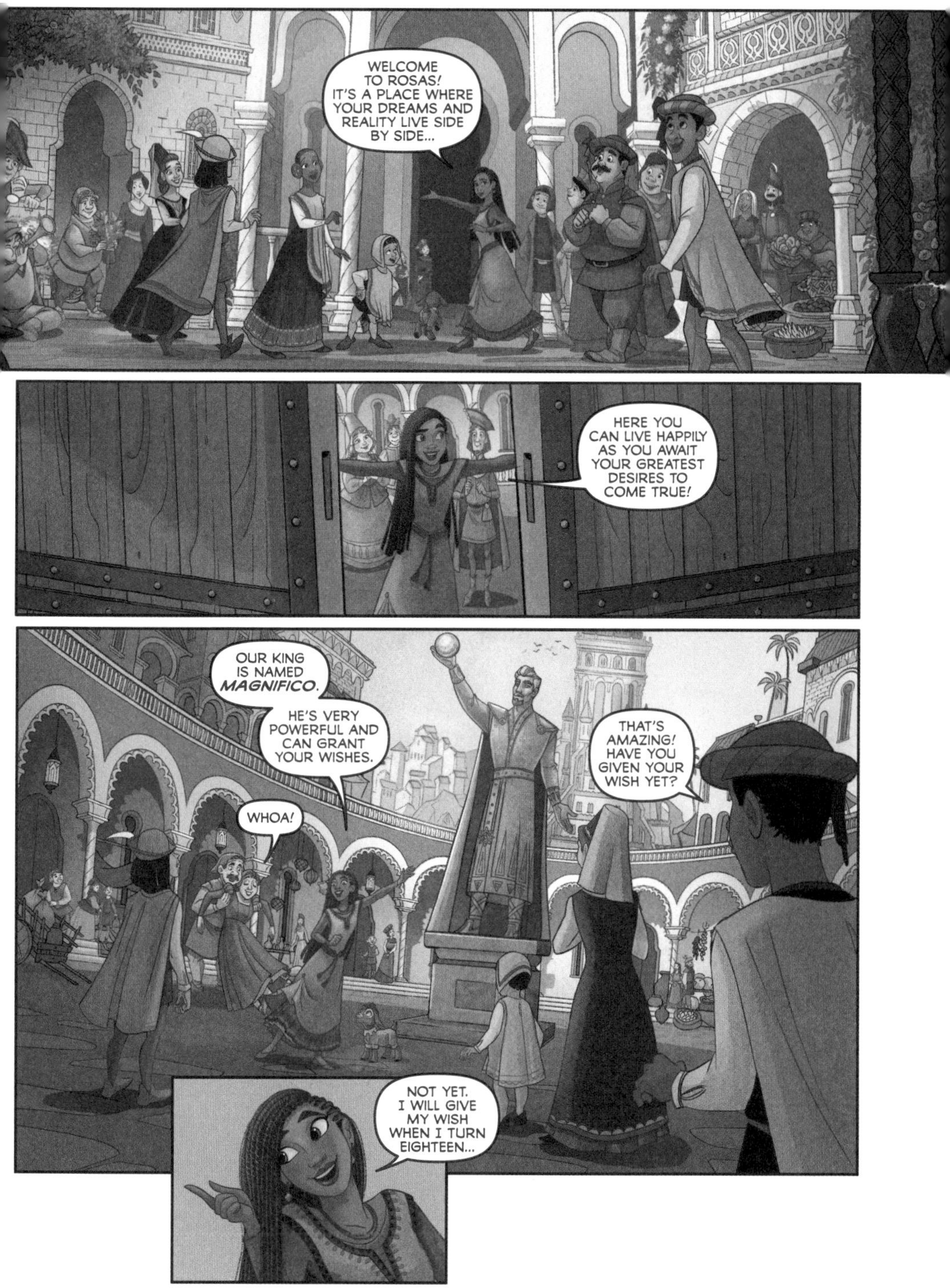
WELCOME TO ROSAS! IT'S A PLACE WHERE YOUR DREAMS AND REALITY LIVE SIDE BY SIDE...
HERE YOU CAN LIVE HAPPILY AS YOU AWAIT YOUR GREATEST DESIRES TO COME TRUE!
OUR KING IS NAMED MAGNIFICO.
HE'S VERY POWERFUL AND CAN GRANT YOUR WISHES.
WHOA!
THAT'S AMAZING! HAVE YOU GIVEN YOUR WISH YET?
NOT YET. I WILL GIVE MY WISH WHEN I TURN EIGHTEEN...

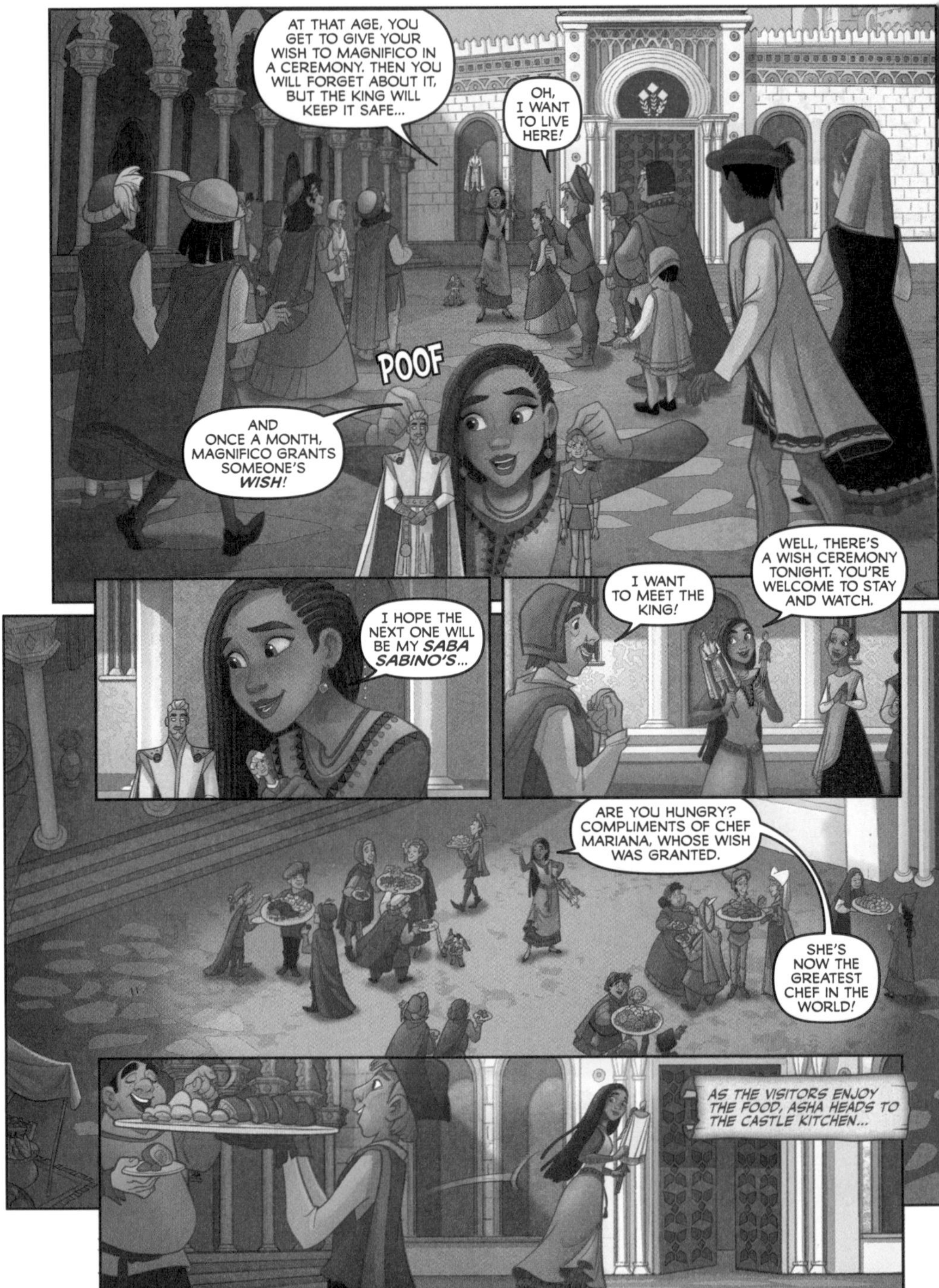
AT THAT AGE, YOU GET TO GIVE YOUR WISH TO MAGNIFICO IN A CEREMONY. THEN YOU WILL FORGET ABOUT IT, BUT THE KING WILL KEEP IT SAFE...
OH, I WANT TO LIVE HERE!
POOF
AND ONCE A MONTH, MAGNIFICO GRANTS SOMEONE'S WISH!
I HOPE THE NEXT ONE WILL BE MY SABA SABINO'S...
I WANT TO MEET THE KING!
WELL, THERE'S A WISH CEREMONY TONIGHT. YOU'RE WELCOME TO STAY AND WATCH.
ARE YOU HUNGRY? COMPLIMENTS OF CHEF MARIANA, WHOSE WISH WAS GRANTED.
SHE'S NOW THE GREATEST CHEF IN THE WORLD!
AS THE VISITORS ENJOY THE FOOD, ASHA HEADS TO THE CASTLE KITCHEN...

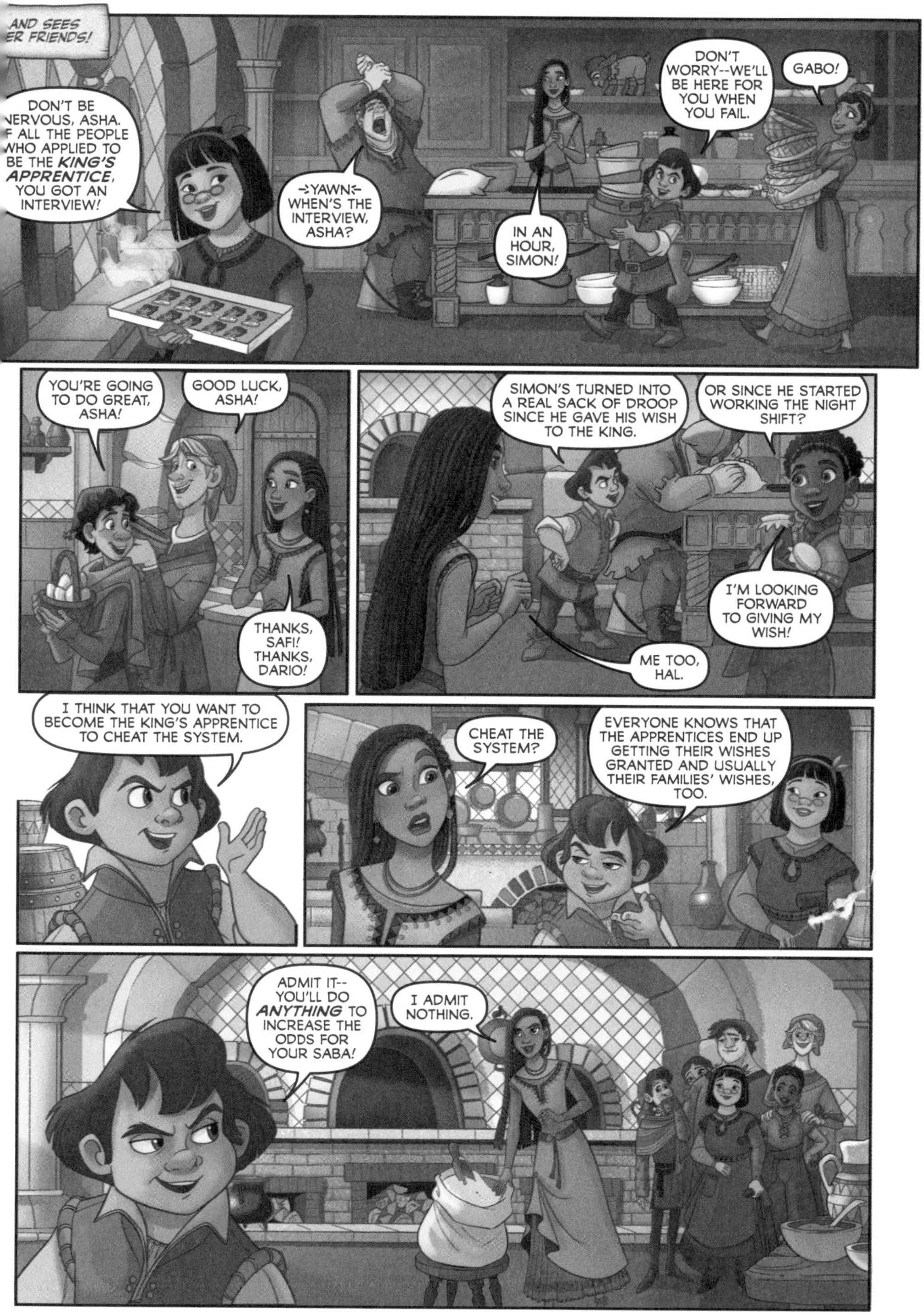

AND SEES ER FRIENDS!
DON'T BE NERVOUS, ASHA. F ALL THE PEOPLE WHO APPLIED TO BE THE *KING'S APPRENTICE*, YOU GOT AN INTERVIEW!
—YAWN— WHEN'S THE INTERVIEW, ASHA?
IN AN HOUR, SIMON!
DON'T WORRY--WE'LL BE HERE FOR YOU WHEN YOU FAIL.
GABO!
YOU'RE GOING TO DO GREAT, ASHA!
GOOD LUCK, ASHA!
THANKS, SAFI! THANKS, DARIO!
SIMON'S TURNED INTO A REAL SACK OF DROOP SINCE HE GAVE HIS WISH TO THE KING.
OR SINCE HE STARTED WORKING THE NIGHT SHIFT?
I'M LOOKING FORWARD TO GIVING MY WISH!
ME TOO, HAL.
I THINK THAT YOU WANT TO BECOME THE KING'S APPRENTICE TO CHEAT THE SYSTEM.
CHEAT THE SYSTEM?
EVERYONE KNOWS THAT THE APPRENTICES END UP GETTING THEIR WISHES GRANTED AND USUALLY THEIR FAMILIES' WISHES, TOO.
ADMIT IT--YOU'LL DO *ANYTHING* TO INCREASE THE ODDS FOR YOUR SABA!
I ADMIT NOTHING.

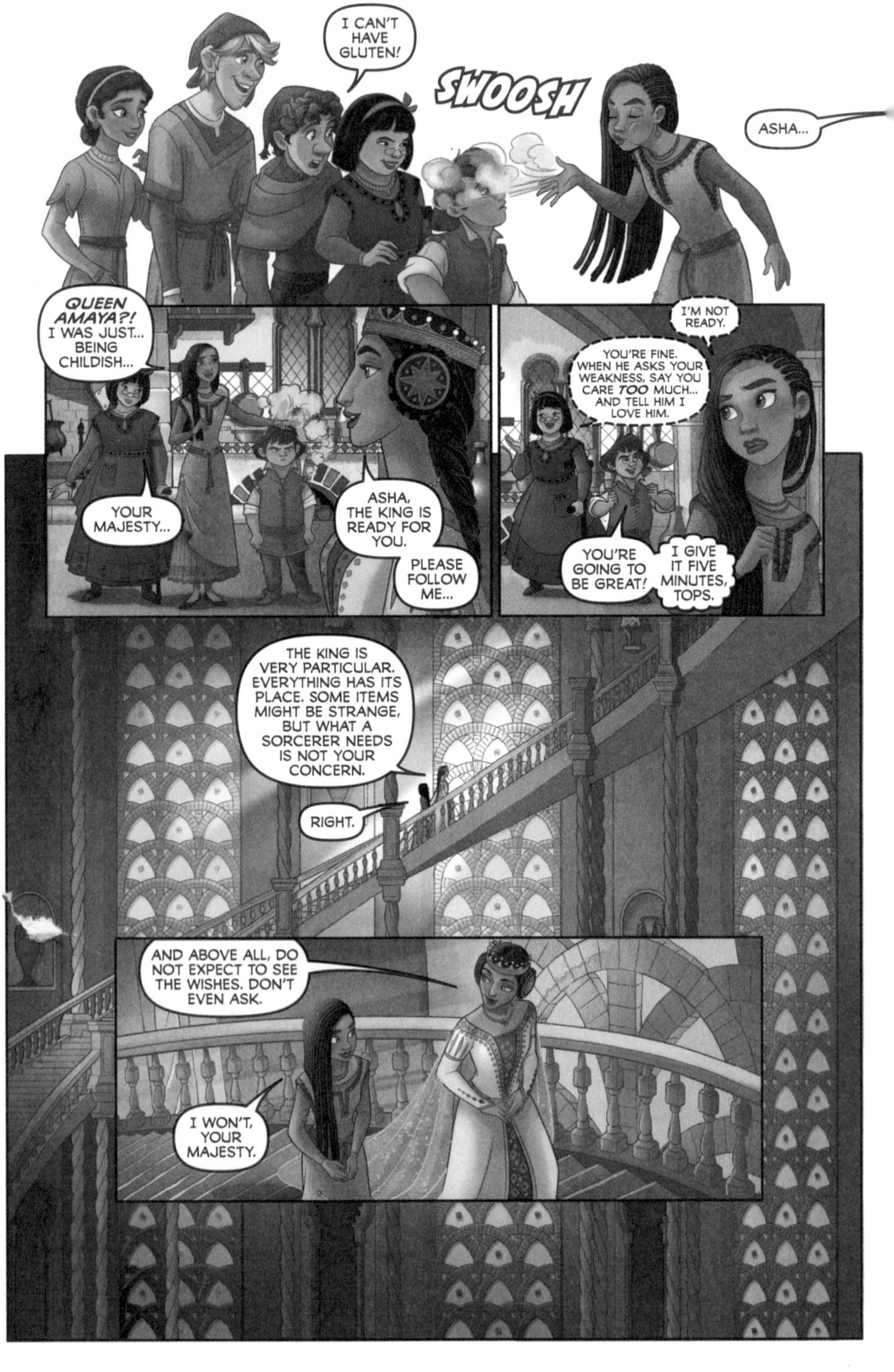
I CAN'T HAVE GLUTEN!
SWOOSH
ASHA...
QUEEN AMAYA?! I WAS JUST... BEING CHILDISH...
YOUR MAJESTY...
ASHA, THE KING IS READY FOR YOU.
PLEASE FOLLOW ME...
I'M NOT READY.
YOU'RE FINE. WHEN HE ASKS YOUR WEAKNESS, SAY YOU CARE *TOO* MUCH... AND TELL HIM I LOVE HIM.
YOU'RE GOING TO BE GREAT!
I GIVE IT FIVE MINUTES, TOPS.
THE KING IS VERY PARTICULAR. EVERYTHING HAS ITS PLACE. SOME ITEMS MIGHT BE STRANGE, BUT WHAT A SORCERER NEEDS IS NOT YOUR CONCERN.
RIGHT.
AND ABOVE ALL, DO NOT EXPECT TO SEE THE WISHES. DON'T EVEN ASK.
I WON'T, YOUR MAJESTY.

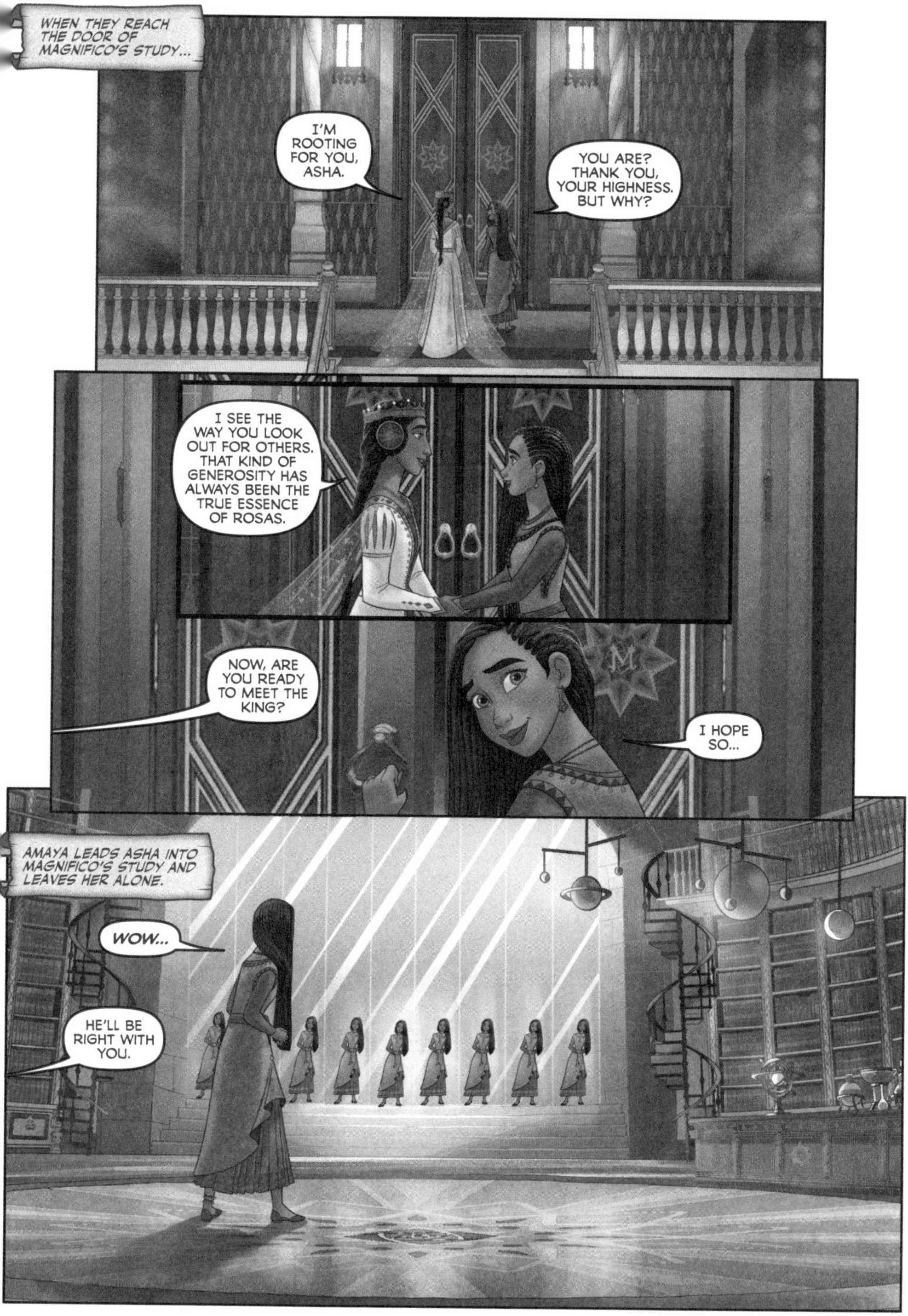
WHEN THEY REACH THE DOOR OF MAGNIFICO'S STUDY...
I'M ROOTING FOR YOU, ASHA.
YOU ARE? THANK YOU, YOUR HIGHNESS. BUT WHY?
I SEE THE WAY YOU LOOK OUT FOR OTHERS. THAT KIND OF GENEROSITY HAS ALWAYS BEEN THE TRUE ESSENCE OF ROSAS.
NOW, ARE YOU READY TO MEET THE KING?
I HOPE SO...
AMAYA LEADS ASHA INTO MAGNIFICO'S STUDY AND LEAVES HER ALONE.
WOW...
HE'LL BE RIGHT WITH YOU.

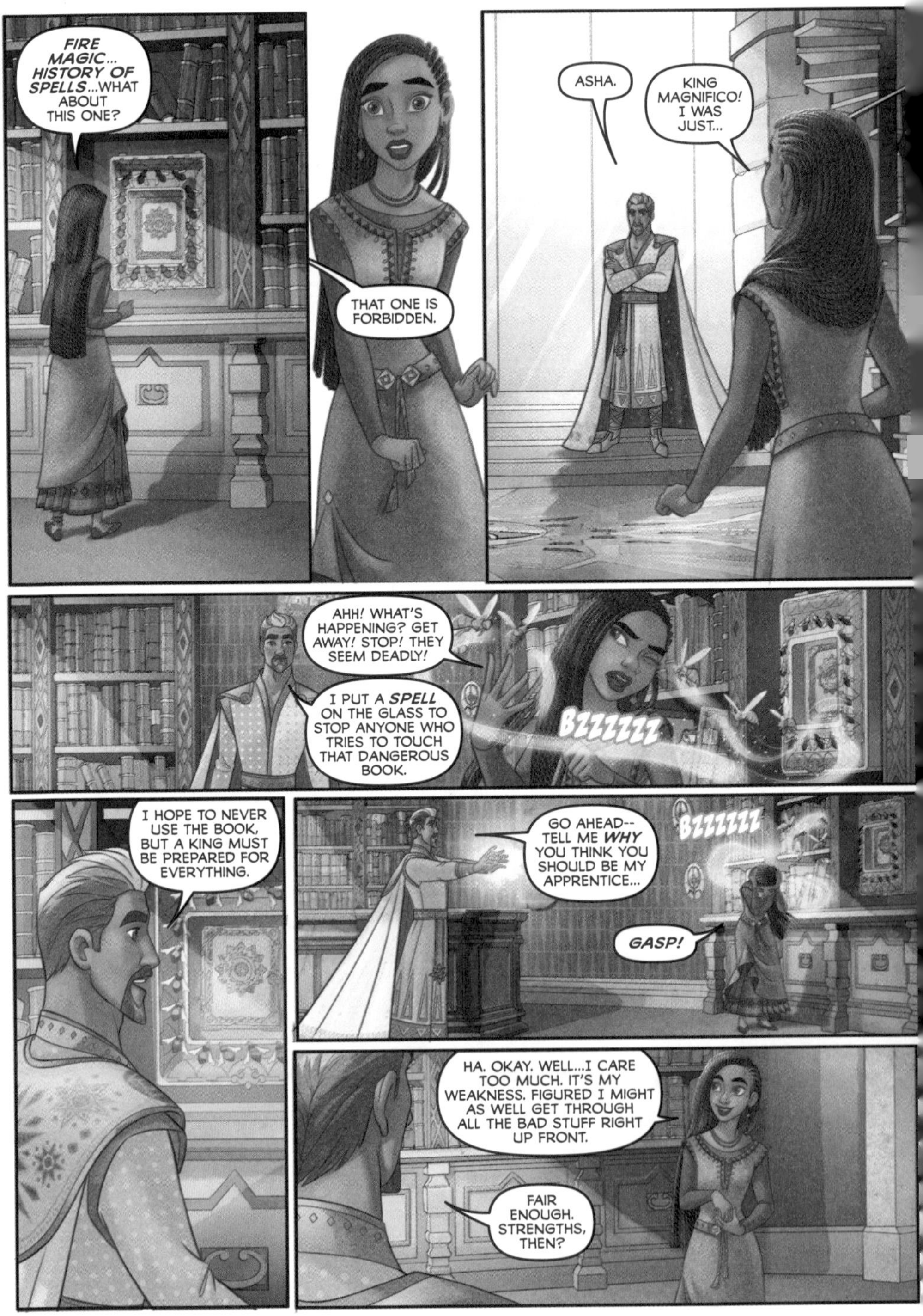

FIRE MAGIC... HISTORY OF SPELLS...WHAT ABOUT THIS ONE?
THAT ONE IS FORBIDDEN.
ASHA.
KING MAGNIFICO! I WAS JUST...
AHH! WHAT'S HAPPENING? GET AWAY! STOP! THEY SEEM DEADLY!
I PUT A SPELL ON THE GLASS TO STOP ANYONE WHO TRIES TO TOUCH THAT DANGEROUS BOOK.
BZZZZZZ
I HOPE TO NEVER USE THE BOOK, BUT A KING MUST BE PREPARED FOR EVERYTHING.
GO AHEAD-- TELL ME WHY YOU THINK YOU SHOULD BE MY APPRENTICE...
BZZZZZZ
GASP!
HA. OKAY. WELL...I CARE TOO MUCH. IT'S MY WEAKNESS. FIGURED I MIGHT AS WELL GET THROUGH ALL THE BAD STUFF RIGHT UP FRONT.
FAIR ENOUGH. STRENGTHS, THEN?

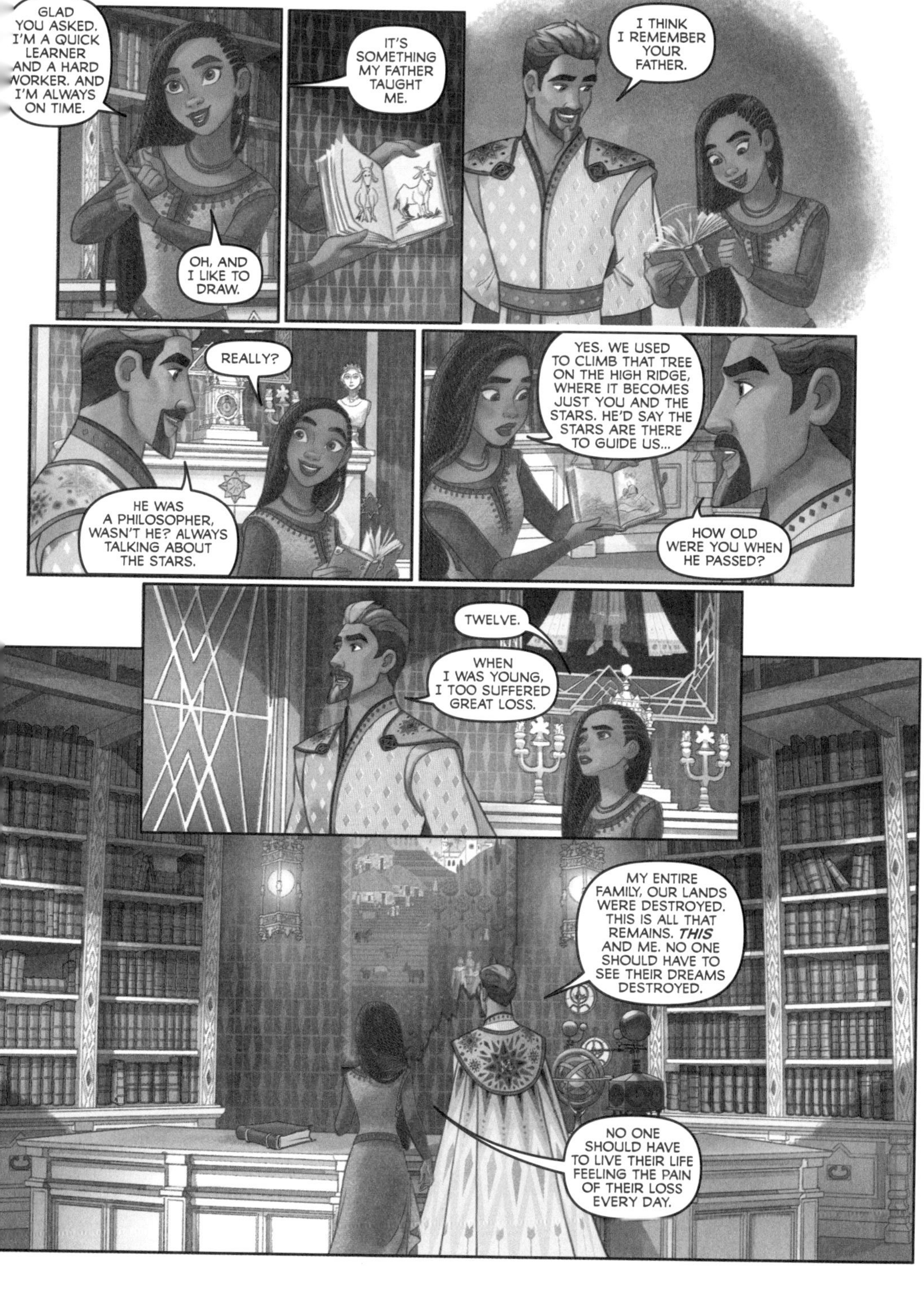
GLAD YOU ASKED. I'M A QUICK LEARNER AND A HARD WORKER. AND I'M ALWAYS ON TIME.
OH, AND I LIKE TO DRAW.
IT'S SOMETHING MY FATHER TAUGHT ME.
I THINK I REMEMBER YOUR FATHER.
REALLY?
HE WAS A PHILOSOPHER, WASN'T HE? ALWAYS TALKING ABOUT THE STARS.
YES. WE USED TO CLIMB THAT TREE ON THE HIGH RIDGE, WHERE IT BECOMES JUST YOU AND THE STARS. HE'D SAY THE STARS ARE THERE TO GUIDE US...
HOW OLD WERE YOU WHEN HE PASSED?
TWELVE.
WHEN I WAS YOUNG, I TOO SUFFERED GREAT LOSS.
MY ENTIRE FAMILY, OUR LANDS WERE DESTROYED. THIS IS ALL THAT REMAINS. *THIS* AND ME. NO ONE SHOULD HAVE TO SEE THEIR DREAMS DESTROYED.
NO ONE SHOULD HAVE TO LIVE THEIR LIFE FEELING THE PAIN OF THEIR LOSS EVERY DAY.

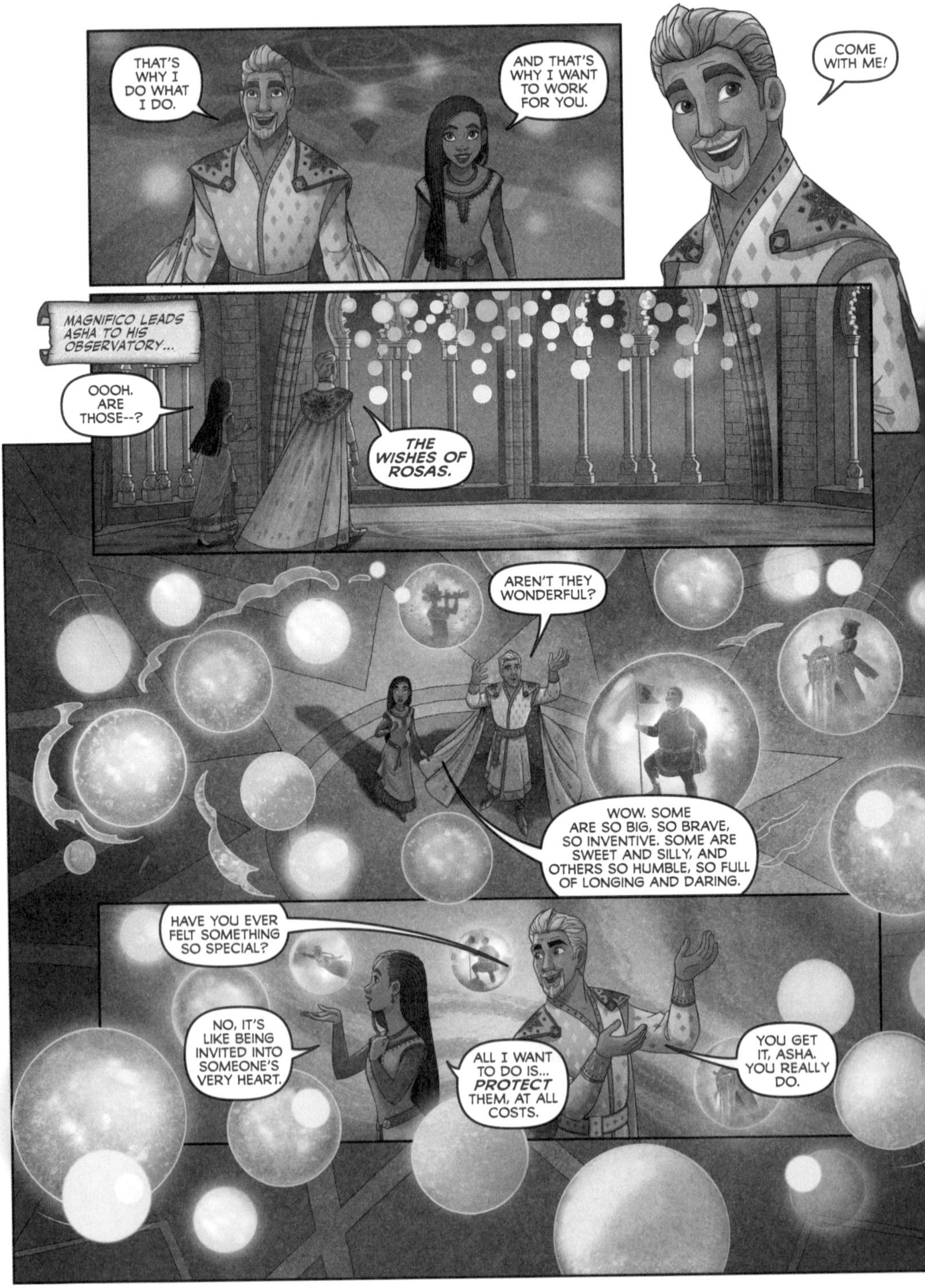
THAT'S WHY I DO WHAT I DO.
AND THAT'S WHY I WANT TO WORK FOR YOU.
COME WITH ME!
MAGNIFICO LEADS ASHA TO HIS OBSERVATORY...
OOOH. ARE THOSE--?
THE WISHES OF ROSAS.
AREN'T THEY WONDERFUL?
WOW. SOME ARE SO BIG, SO BRAVE, SO INVENTIVE. SOME ARE SWEET AND SILLY, AND OTHERS SO HUMBLE, SO FULL OF LONGING AND DARING.
HAVE YOU EVER FELT SOMETHING SO SPECIAL?
NO, IT'S LIKE BEING INVITED INTO SOMEONE'S VERY HEART.
ALL I WANT TO DO IS... PROTECT THEM, AT ALL COSTS.
YOU GET IT, ASHA. YOU REALLY DO.

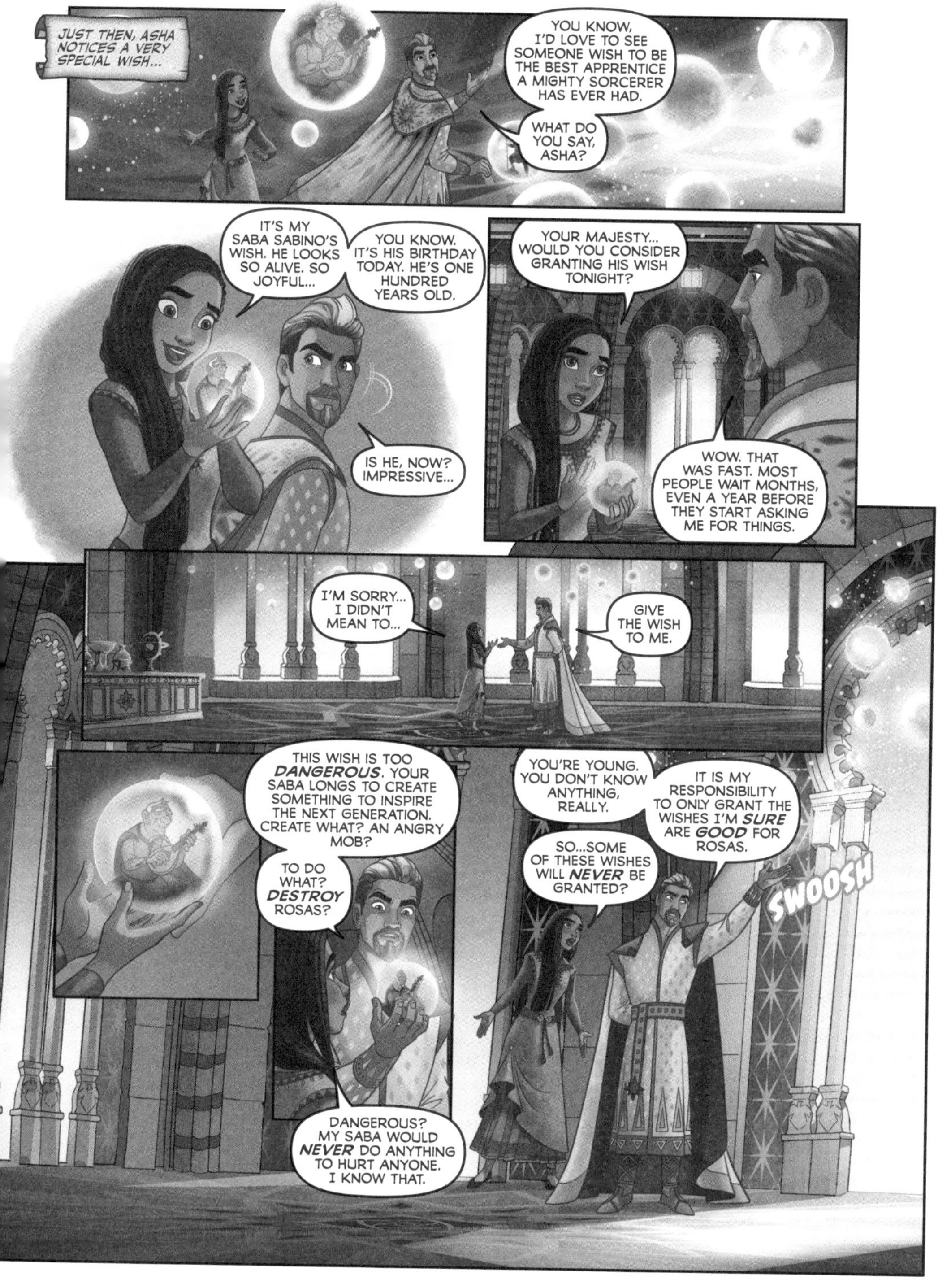
JUST THEN, ASHA NOTICES A VERY SPECIAL WISH...
YOU KNOW, I'D LOVE TO SEE SOMEONE WISH TO BE THE BEST APPRENTICE A MIGHTY SORCERER HAS EVER HAD.
WHAT DO YOU SAY, ASHA?
IT'S MY SABA SABINO'S WISH. HE LOOKS SO ALIVE. SO JOYFUL...
YOU KNOW. IT'S HIS BIRTHDAY TODAY. HE'S ONE HUNDRED YEARS OLD.
IS HE, NOW? IMPRESSIVE...
YOUR MAJESTY... WOULD YOU CONSIDER GRANTING HIS WISH TONIGHT?
WOW. THAT WAS FAST. MOST PEOPLE WAIT MONTHS, EVEN A YEAR BEFORE THEY START ASKING ME FOR THINGS.
I'M SORRY... I DIDN'T MEAN TO...
GIVE THE WISH TO ME.
THIS WISH IS TOO **DANGEROUS**. YOUR SABA LONGS TO CREATE SOMETHING TO INSPIRE THE NEXT GENERATION. CREATE WHAT? AN ANGRY MOB?
TO DO WHAT? **DESTROY** ROSAS?
DANGEROUS? MY SABA WOULD **NEVER** DO ANYTHING TO HURT ANYONE. I KNOW THAT.
YOU'RE YOUNG. YOU DON'T KNOW ANYTHING, REALLY.
IT IS MY RESPONSIBILITY TO ONLY GRANT THE WISHES I'M **SURE** ARE **GOOD** FOR ROSAS.
SO...SOME OF THESE WISHES WILL **NEVER** BE GRANTED?
SWOOSH

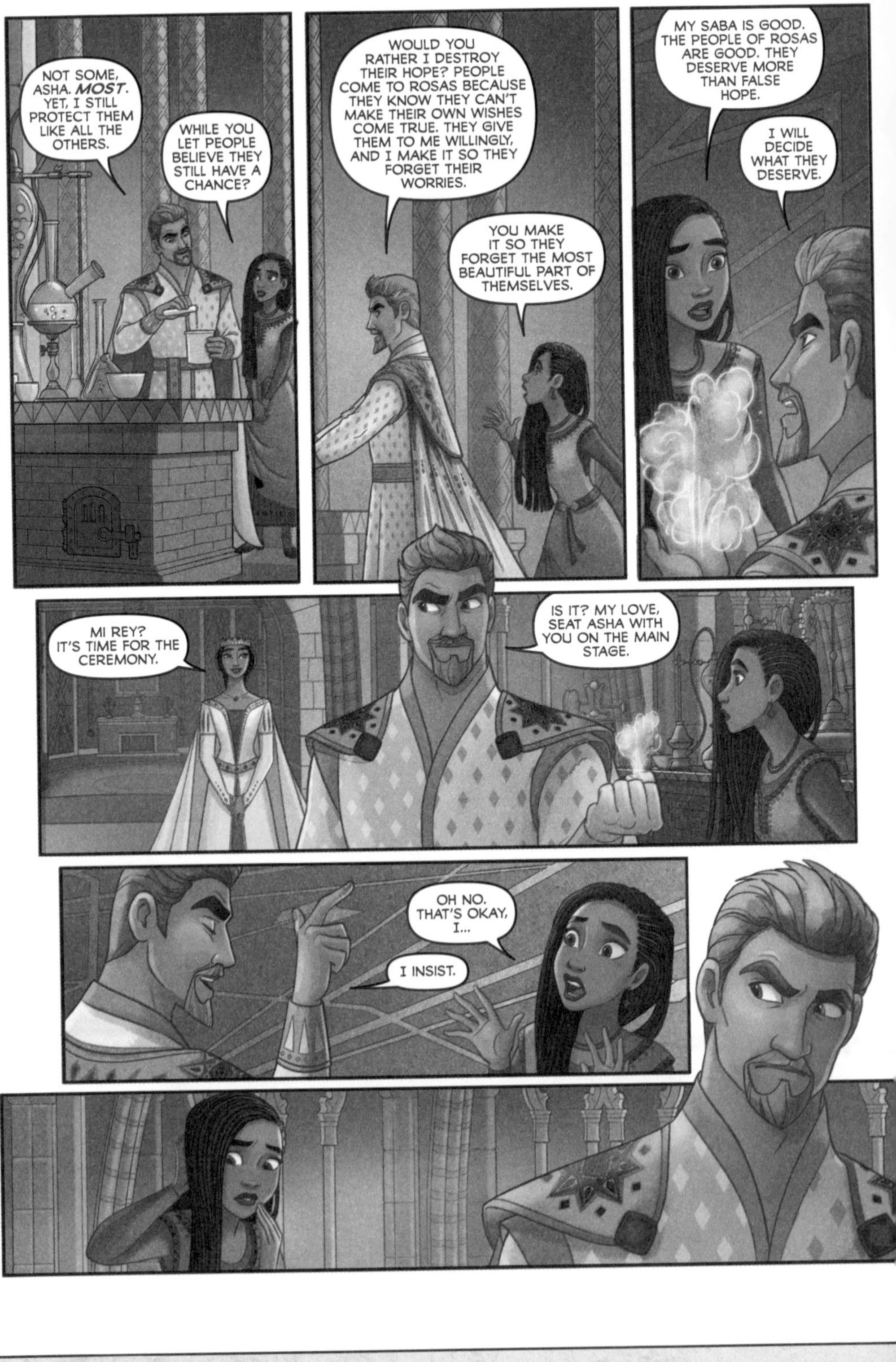
NOT SOME, ASHA. **MOST**. YET, I STILL PROTECT THEM LIKE ALL THE OTHERS.
WHILE YOU LET PEOPLE BELIEVE THEY STILL HAVE A CHANCE?
WOULD YOU RATHER I DESTROY THEIR HOPE? PEOPLE COME TO ROSAS BECAUSE THEY KNOW THEY CAN'T MAKE THEIR OWN WISHES COME TRUE. THEY GIVE THEM TO ME WILLINGLY, AND I MAKE IT SO THEY FORGET THEIR WORRIES.
YOU MAKE IT SO THEY FORGET THE MOST BEAUTIFUL PART OF THEMSELVES.
MY SABA IS GOOD. THE PEOPLE OF ROSAS ARE GOOD. THEY DESERVE MORE THAN FALSE HOPE.
I WILL DECIDE WHAT THEY DESERVE.
MI REY? IT'S TIME FOR THE CEREMONY.
IS IT? MY LOVE, SEAT ASHA WITH YOU ON THE MAIN STAGE.
OH NO. THAT'S OKAY, I...
I INSIST.

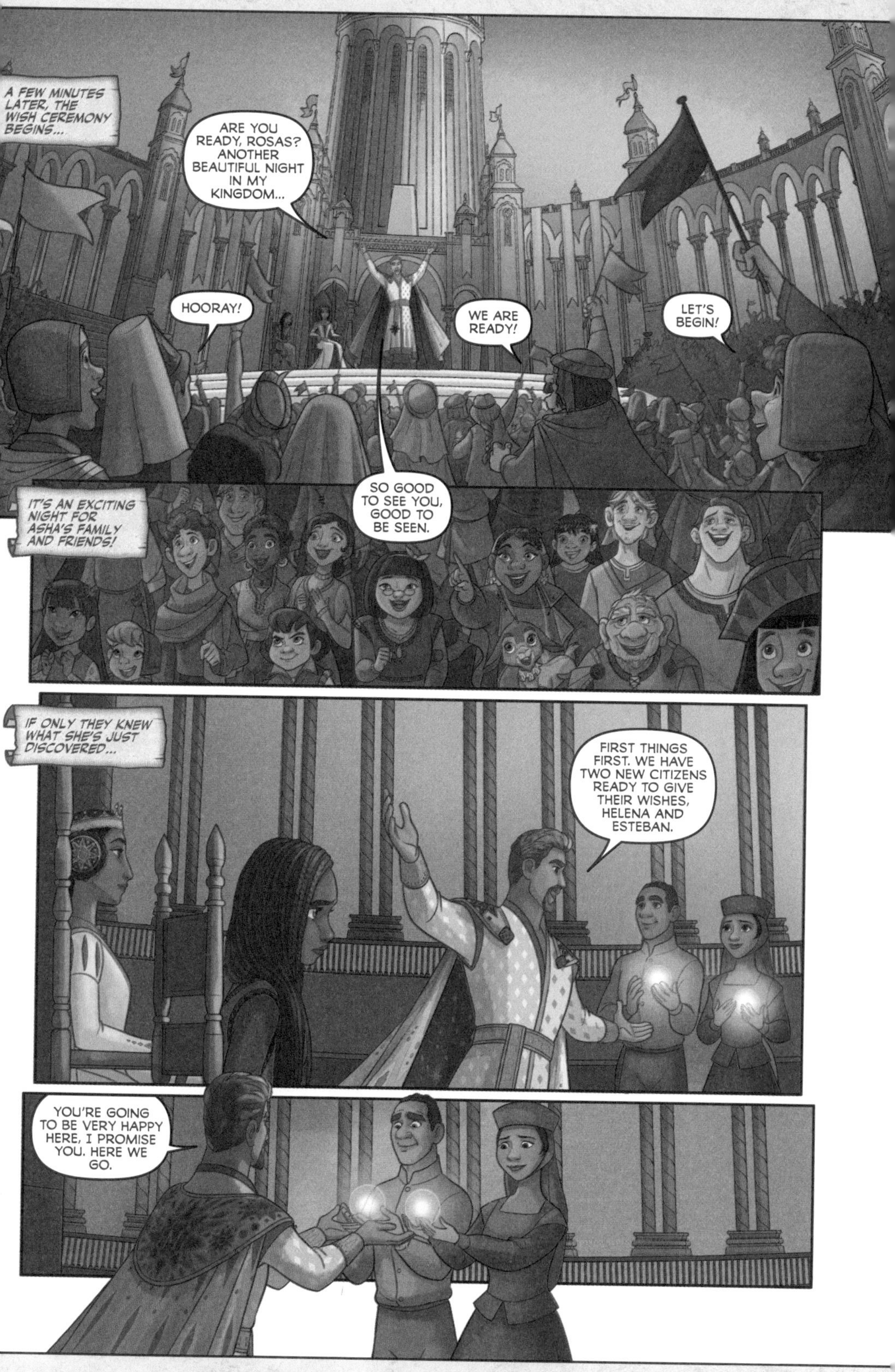
A FEW MINUTES LATER, THE WISH CEREMONY BEGINS...
ARE YOU READY, ROSAS? ANOTHER BEAUTIFUL NIGHT IN MY KINGDOM...
HOORAY!
WE ARE READY!
LET'S BEGIN!
SO GOOD TO SEE YOU, GOOD TO BE SEEN.
IT'S AN EXCITING NIGHT FOR ASHA'S FAMILY AND FRIENDS!
IF ONLY THEY KNEW WHAT SHE'S JUST DISCOVERED...
FIRST THINGS FIRST. WE HAVE TWO NEW CITIZENS READY TO GIVE THEIR WISHES, HELENA AND ESTEBAN.
YOU'RE GOING TO BE VERY HAPPY HERE, I PROMISE YOU. HERE WE GO.

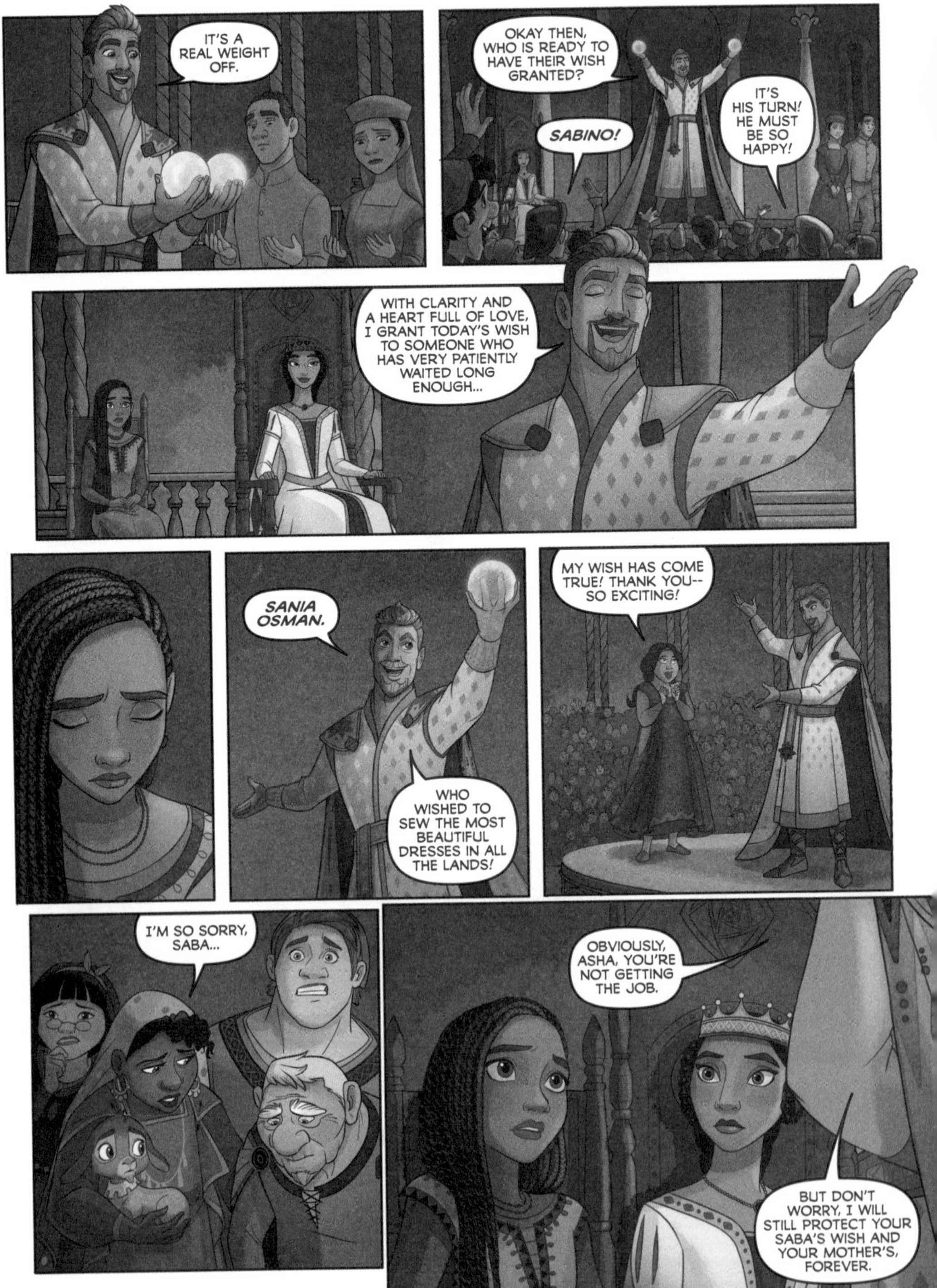
IT'S A REAL WEIGHT OFF.
OKAY THEN, WHO IS READY TO HAVE THEIR WISH GRANTED?
SABINO!
IT'S HIS TURN! HE MUST BE SO HAPPY!
WITH CLARITY AND A HEART FULL OF LOVE, I GRANT TODAY'S WISH TO SOMEONE WHO HAS VERY PATIENTLY WAITED LONG ENOUGH...
SANIA OSMAN.
WHO WISHED TO SEW THE MOST BEAUTIFUL DRESSES IN ALL THE LANDS!
MY WISH HAS COME TRUE! THANK YOU-- SO EXCITING!
I'M SO SORRY, SABA...
OBVIOUSLY, ASHA, YOU'RE NOT GETTING THE JOB.
BUT DON'T WORRY, I WILL STILL PROTECT YOUR SABA'S WISH AND YOUR MOTHER'S, FOREVER.

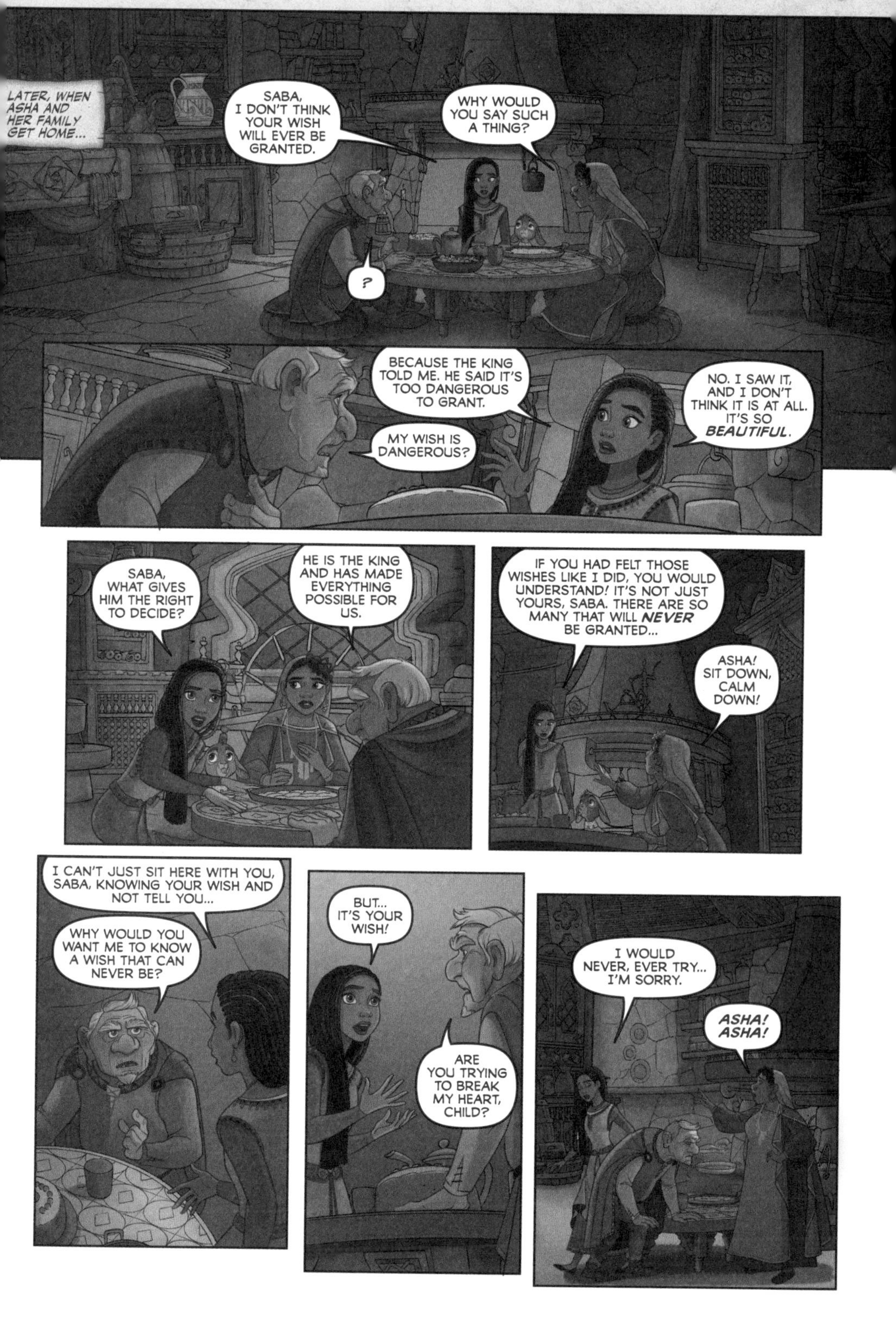

LATER, WHEN ASHA AND HER FAMILY GET HOME...
SABA, I DON'T THINK YOUR WISH WILL EVER BE GRANTED.
WHY WOULD YOU SAY SUCH A THING?
?
BECAUSE THE KING TOLD ME. HE SAID IT'S TOO DANGEROUS TO GRANT.
MY WISH IS DANGEROUS?
NO. I SAW IT, AND I DON'T THINK IT IS AT ALL. IT'S SO ***BEAUTIFUL***.
SABA, WHAT GIVES HIM THE RIGHT TO DECIDE?
HE IS THE KING AND HAS MADE EVERYTHING POSSIBLE FOR US.
IF YOU HAD FELT THOSE WISHES LIKE I DID, YOU WOULD UNDERSTAND! IT'S NOT JUST YOURS, SABA. THERE ARE SO MANY THAT WILL ***NEVER*** BE GRANTED...
ASHA! SIT DOWN, CALM DOWN!
I CAN'T JUST SIT HERE WITH YOU, SABA, KNOWING YOUR WISH AND NOT TELL YOU...
WHY WOULD YOU WANT ME TO KNOW A WISH THAT CAN NEVER BE?
BUT... IT'S YOUR WISH!
ARE YOU TRYING TO BREAK MY HEART, CHILD?
I WOULD NEVER, EVER TRY... I'M SORRY.
ASHA! ASHA!

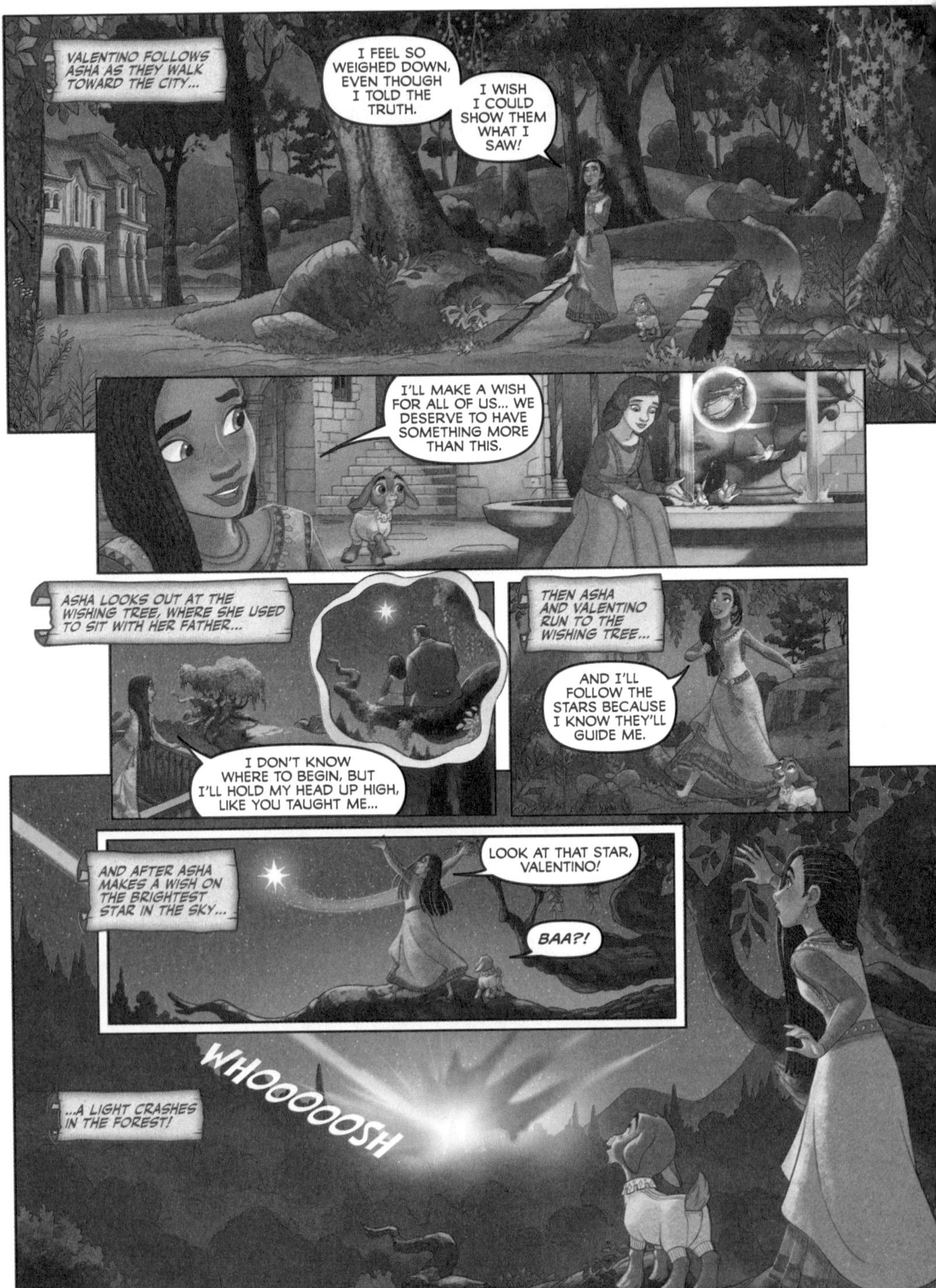
VALENTINO FOLLOWS ASHA AS THEY WALK TOWARD THE CITY...
I FEEL SO WEIGHED DOWN, EVEN THOUGH I TOLD THE TRUTH.
I WISH I COULD SHOW THEM WHAT I SAW!
I'LL MAKE A WISH FOR ALL OF US... WE DESERVE TO HAVE SOMETHING MORE THAN THIS.
ASHA LOOKS OUT AT THE WISHING TREE, WHERE SHE USED TO SIT WITH HER FATHER...
I DON'T KNOW WHERE TO BEGIN, BUT I'LL HOLD MY HEAD UP HIGH, LIKE YOU TAUGHT ME...
THEN ASHA AND VALENTINO RUN TO THE WISHING TREE...
AND I'LL FOLLOW THE STARS BECAUSE I KNOW THEY'LL GUIDE ME.
AND AFTER ASHA MAKES A WISH ON THE BRIGHTEST STAR IN THE SKY...
LOOK AT THAT STAR, VALENTINO!
BAA?!
WHOOOOOSH
...A LIGHT CRASHES IN THE FOREST!

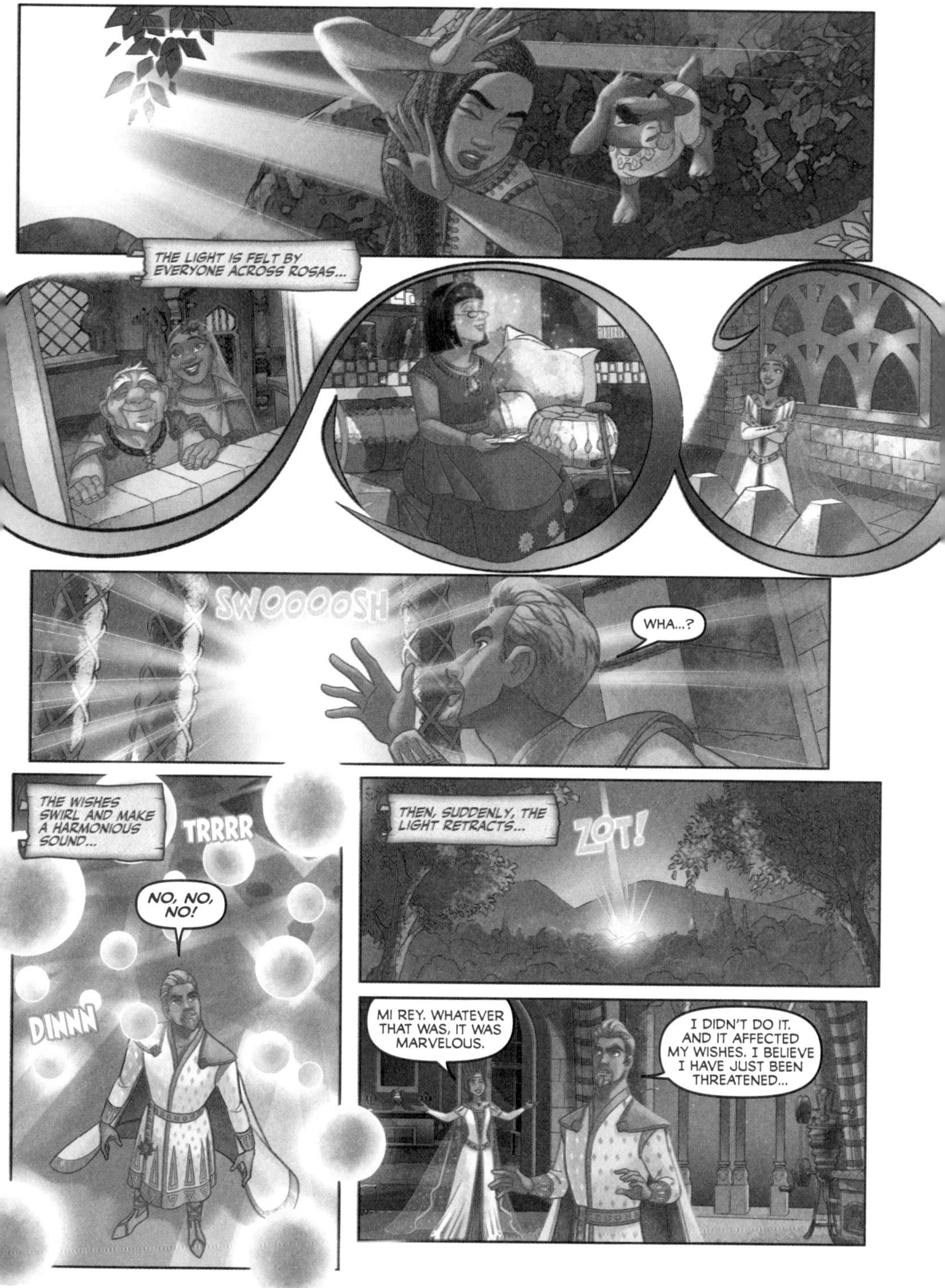
THE LIGHT IS FELT BY EVERYONE ACROSS ROSAS...
SWOOOOSH
WHA...?
THE WISHES SWIRL AND MAKE A HARMONIOUS SOUND...
TRRRR
NO, NO, NO!
DINNN
THEN, SUDDENLY, THE LIGHT RETRACTS...
ZOT!
MI REY. WHATEVER THAT WAS, IT WAS MARVELOUS.
I DIDN'T DO IT. AND IT AFFECTED MY WISHES. I BELIEVE I HAVE JUST BEEN THREATENED...

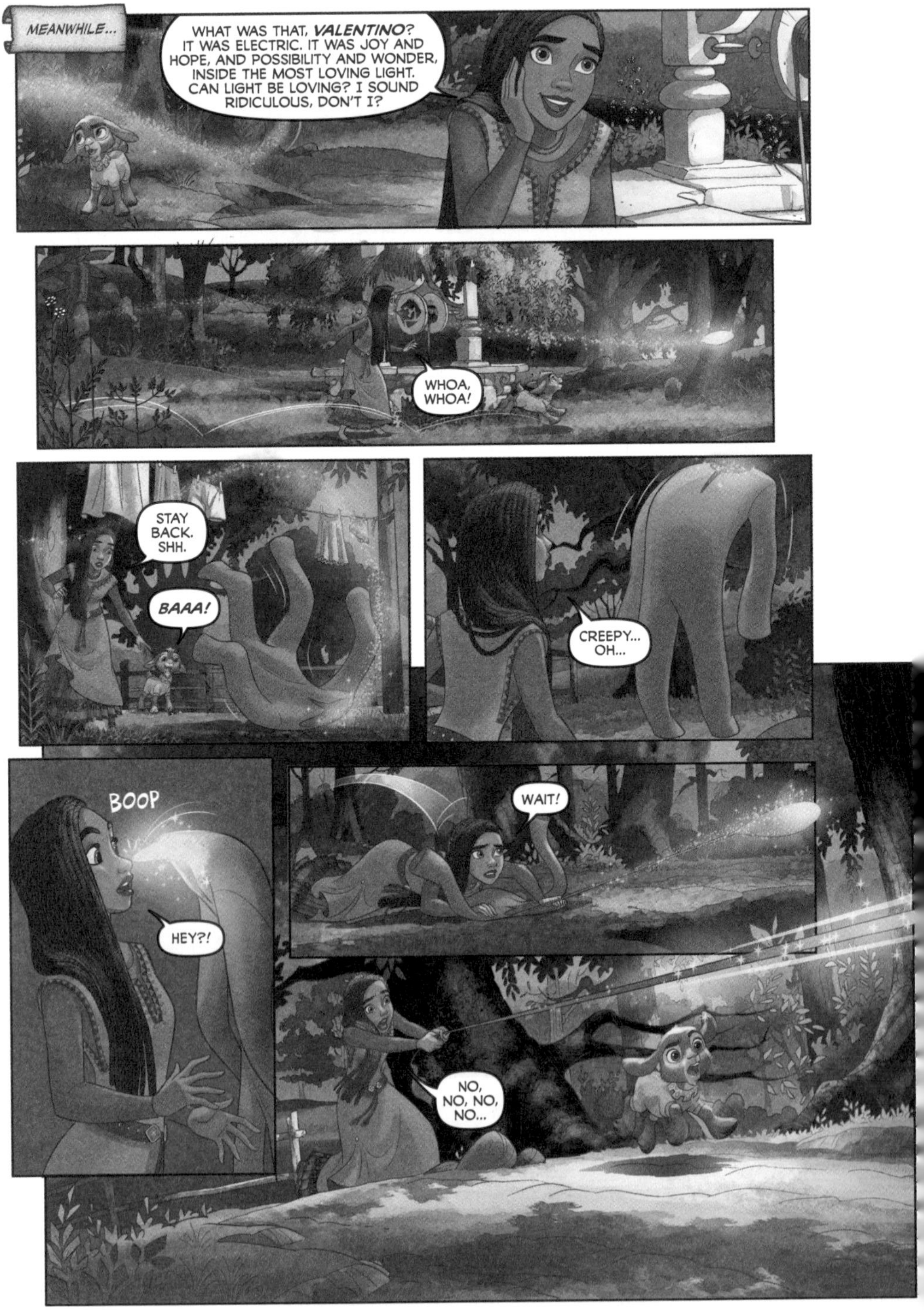
MEANWHILE...
WHAT WAS THAT, VALENTINO? IT WAS ELECTRIC. IT WAS JOY AND HOPE, AND POSSIBILITY AND WONDER, INSIDE THE MOST LOVING LIGHT. CAN LIGHT BE LOVING? I SOUND RIDICULOUS, DON'T I?
WHOA, WHOA!
STAY BACK. SHH.
BAAA!
CREEPY... OH...
BOOP
HEY?!
WAIT!
NO, NO, NO, NO...

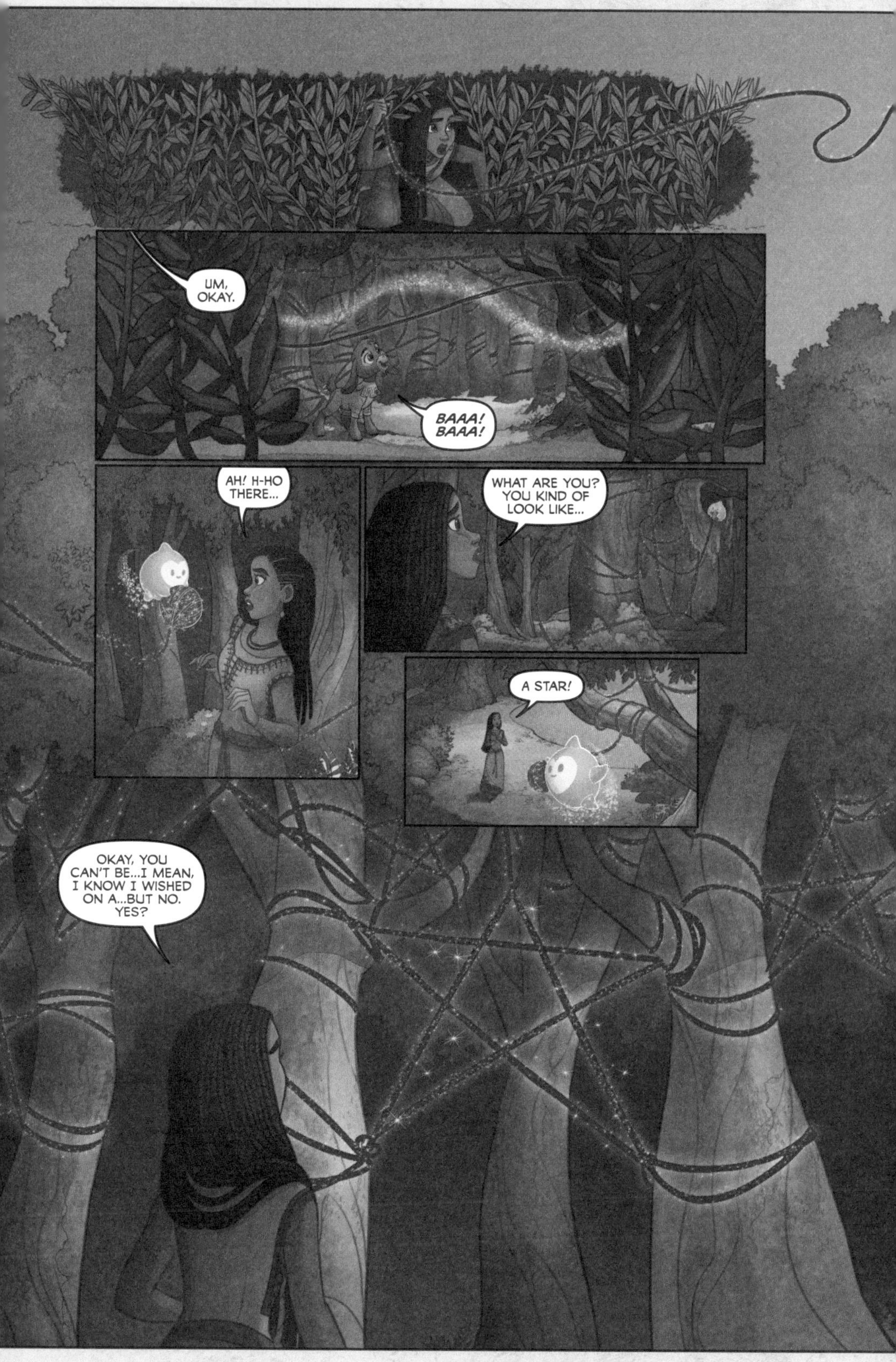
UM, OKAY.
BAAA! BAAA!
AH! H-HO THERE...
WHAT ARE YOU? YOU KIND OF LOOK LIKE...
A STAR!
OKAY, YOU CAN'T BE...I MEAN, I KNOW I WISHED ON A...BUT NO. YES?

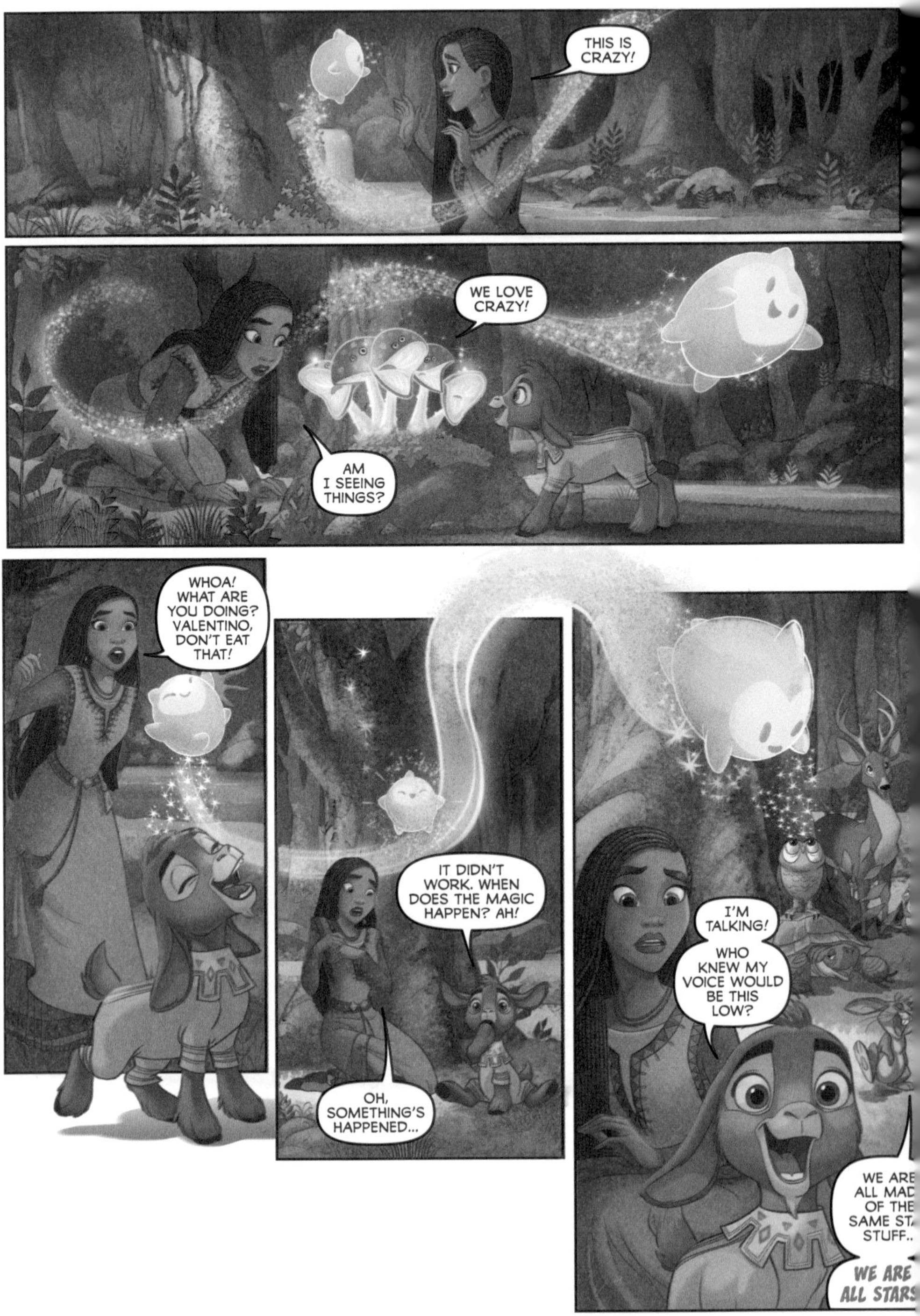
THIS IS CRAZY!
WE LOVE CRAZY!
AM I SEEING THINGS?
WHOA! WHAT ARE YOU DOING? VALENTINO, DON'T EAT THAT!
IT DIDN'T WORK. WHEN DOES THE MAGIC HAPPEN? AH!
OH, SOMETHING'S HAPPENED...
I'M TALKING!
WHO KNEW MY VOICE WOULD BE THIS LOW?
WE ARE ALL MAD OF THE SAME STA STUFF..
WE ARE ALL STARS

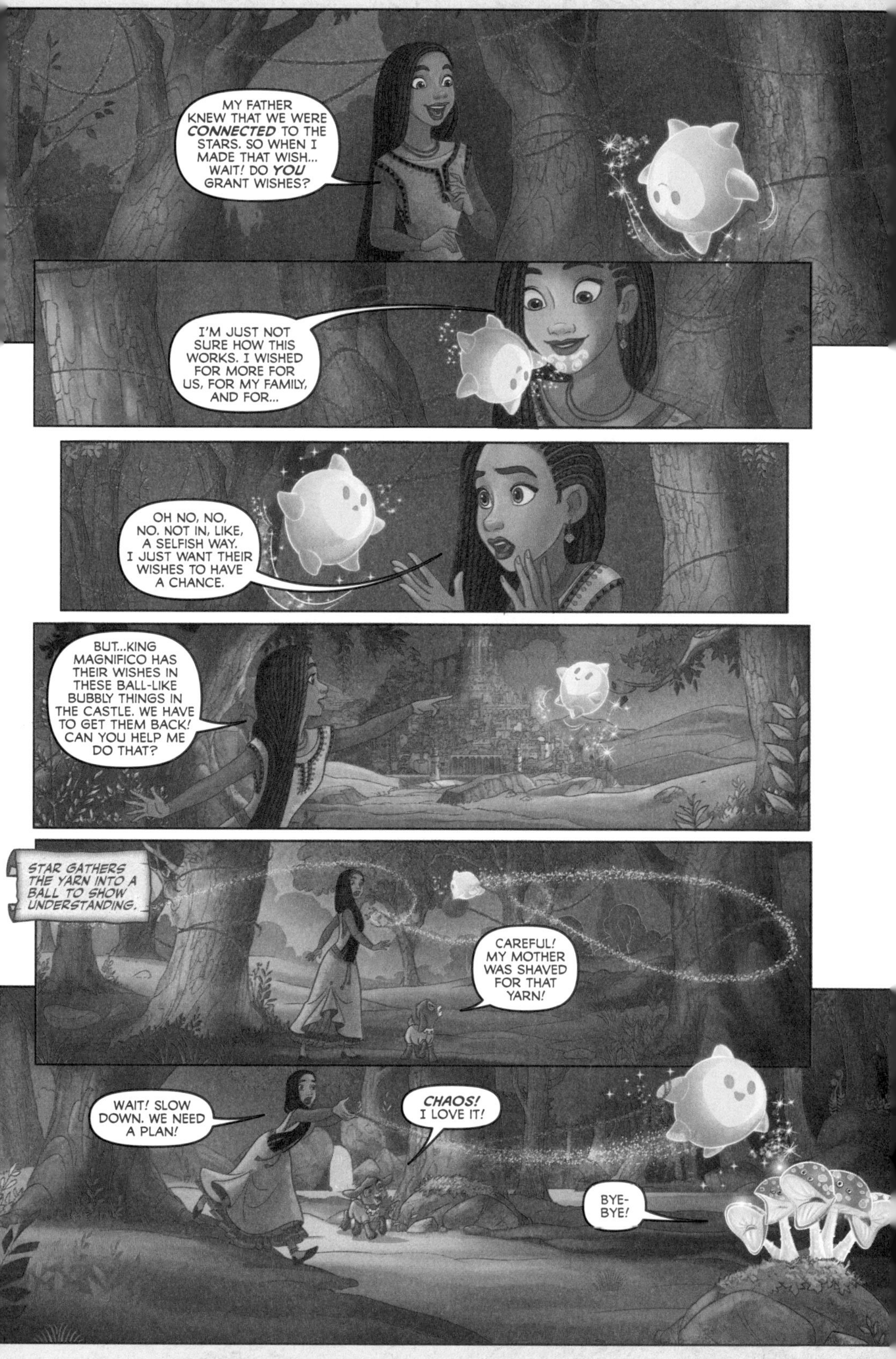
MY FATHER KNEW THAT WE WERE CONNECTED TO THE STARS. SO WHEN I MADE THAT WISH... WAIT! DO YOU GRANT WISHES?
I'M JUST NOT SURE HOW THIS WORKS. I WISHED FOR MORE FOR US, FOR MY FAMILY, AND FOR...
OH NO, NO, NO. NOT IN, LIKE, A SELFISH WAY. I JUST WANT THEIR WISHES TO HAVE A CHANCE.
BUT...KING MAGNIFICO HAS THEIR WISHES IN THESE BALL-LIKE BUBBLY THINGS IN THE CASTLE. WE HAVE TO GET THEM BACK! CAN YOU HELP ME DO THAT?
STAR GATHERS THE YARN INTO A BALL TO SHOW UNDERSTANDING.
CAREFUL! MY MOTHER WAS SHAVED FOR THAT YARN!
WAIT! SLOW DOWN. WE NEED A PLAN!
CHAOS! I LOVE IT!
BYE-BYE!

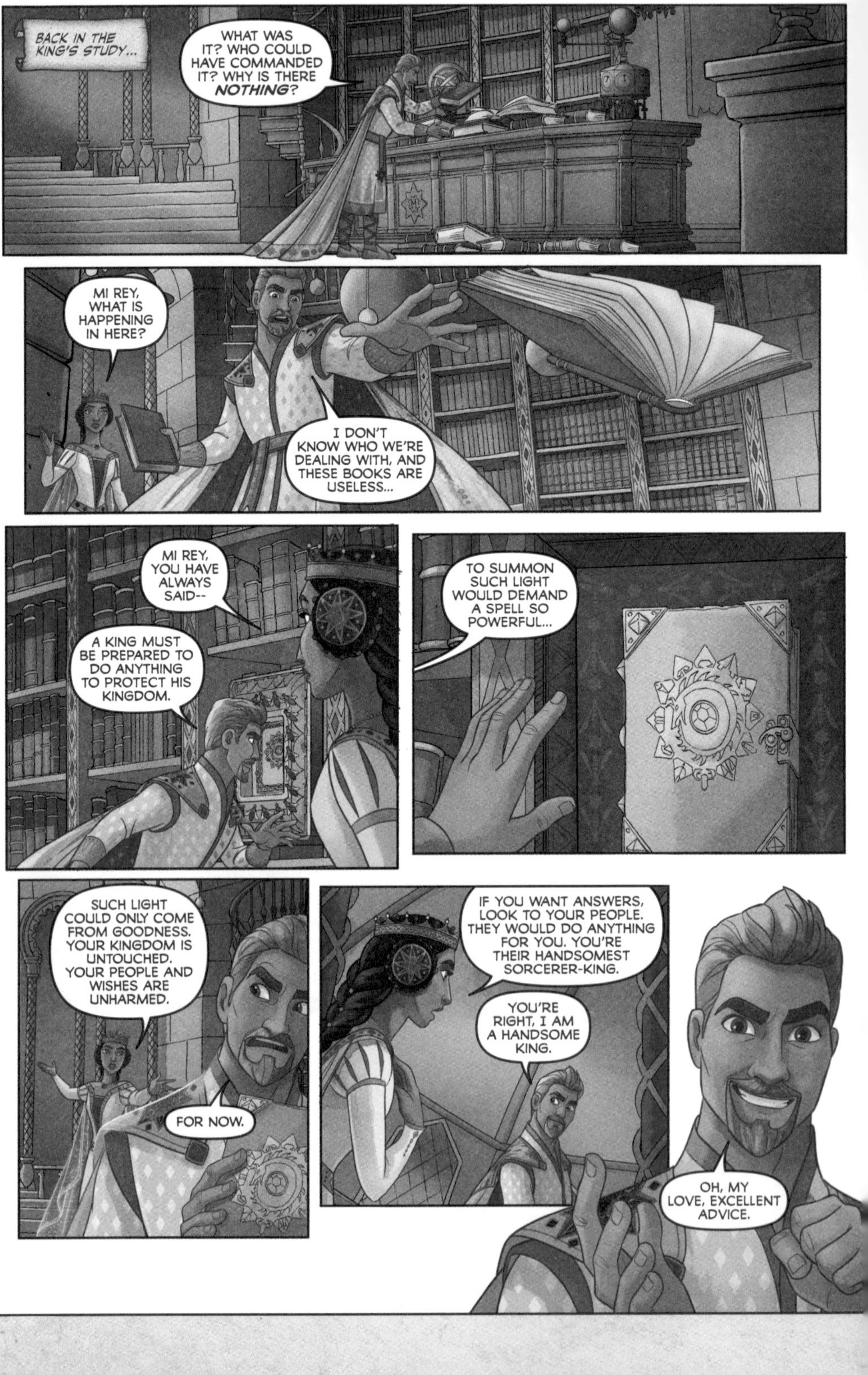
BACK IN THE KING'S STUDY...
WHAT WAS IT? WHO COULD HAVE COMMANDED IT? WHY IS THERE ***NOTHING***?
MI REY, WHAT IS HAPPENING IN HERE?
I DON'T KNOW WHO WE'RE DEALING WITH, AND THESE BOOKS ARE USELESS...
MI REY, YOU HAVE ALWAYS SAID--
A KING MUST BE PREPARED TO DO ANYTHING TO PROTECT HIS KINGDOM.
TO SUMMON SUCH LIGHT WOULD DEMAND A SPELL SO POWERFUL...
SUCH LIGHT COULD ONLY COME FROM GOODNESS. YOUR KINGDOM IS UNTOUCHED. YOUR PEOPLE AND WISHES ARE UNHARMED.
FOR NOW.
IF YOU WANT ANSWERS, LOOK TO YOUR PEOPLE. THEY WOULD DO ANYTHING FOR YOU. YOU'RE THEIR HANDSOMEST SORCERER-KING.
YOU'RE RIGHT, I AM A HANDSOME KING.
OH, MY LOVE, EXCELLENT ADVICE.

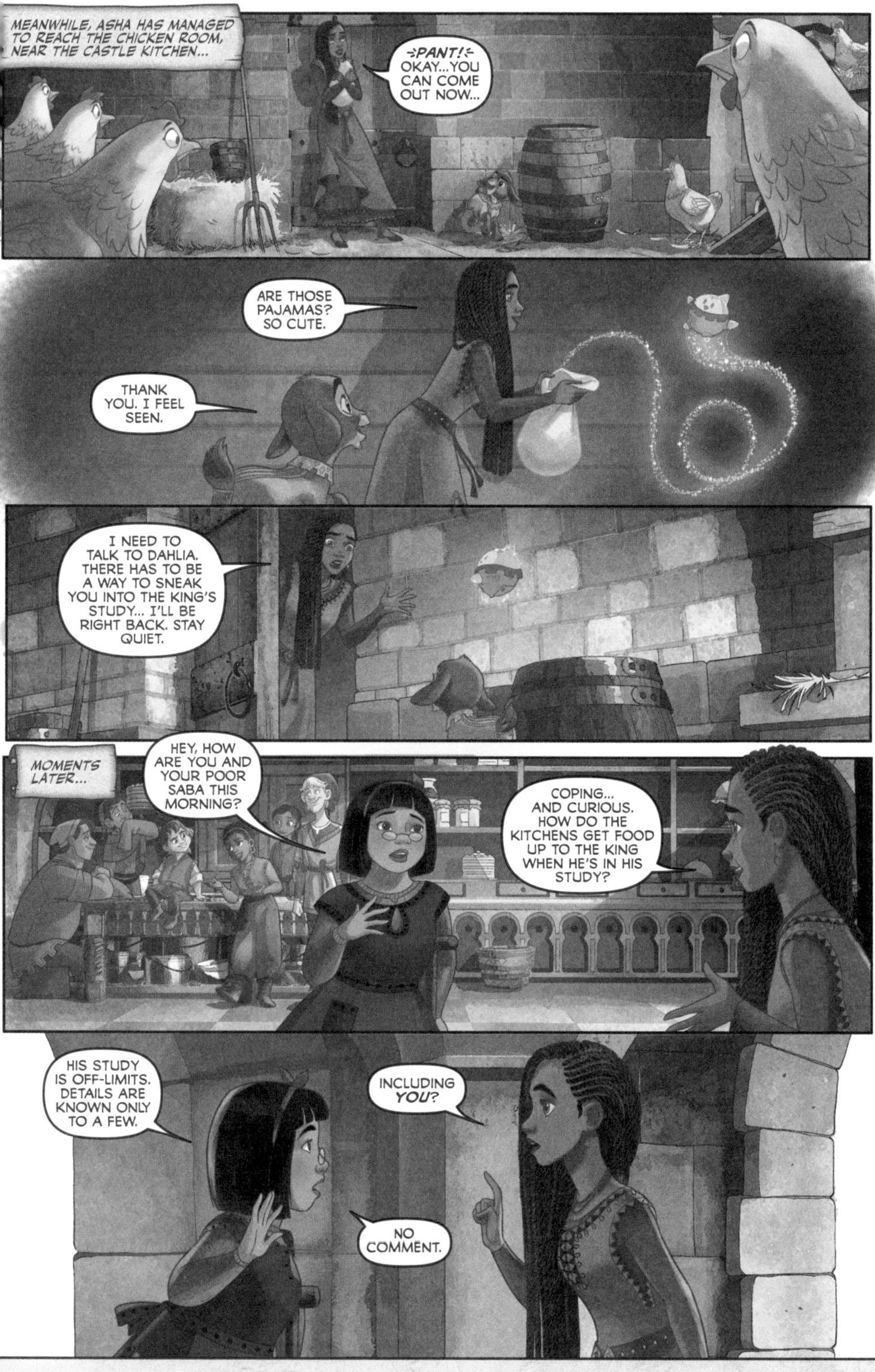
MEANWHILE, ASHA HAS MANAGED TO REACH THE CHICKEN ROOM, NEAR THE CASTLE KITCHEN...
PANT! OKAY...YOU CAN COME OUT NOW...
ARE THOSE PAJAMAS? SO CUTE.
THANK YOU. I FEEL SEEN.
I NEED TO TALK TO DAHLIA. THERE HAS TO BE A WAY TO SNEAK YOU INTO THE KING'S STUDY... I'LL BE RIGHT BACK. STAY QUIET.
MOMENTS LATER...
HEY, HOW ARE YOU AND YOUR POOR SABA THIS MORNING?
COPING... AND CURIOUS. HOW DO THE KITCHENS GET FOOD UP TO THE KING WHEN HE'S IN HIS STUDY?
HIS STUDY IS OFF-LIMITS. DETAILS ARE KNOWN ONLY TO A FEW.
INCLUDING *YOU*?
NO COMMENT.

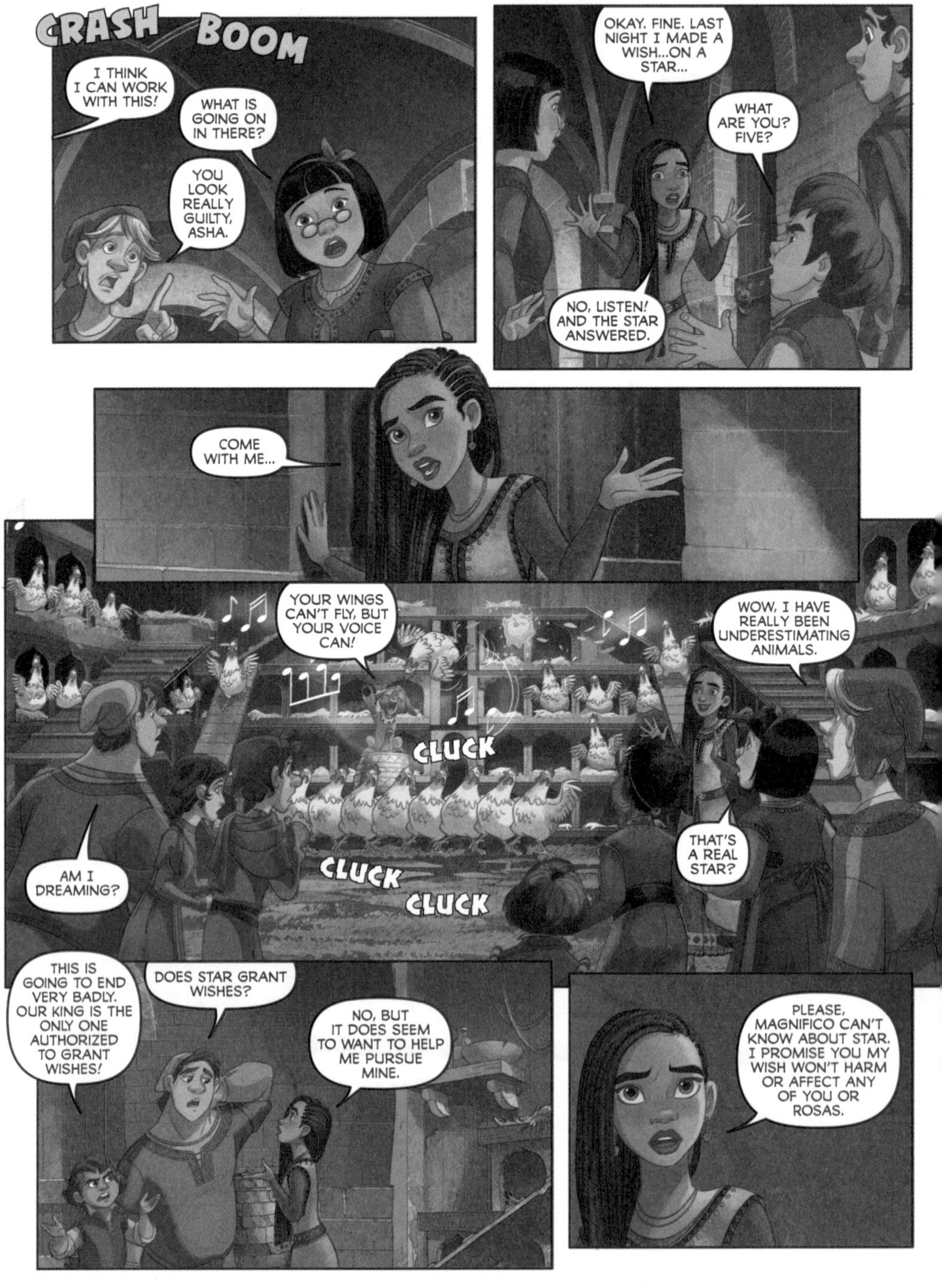
CRASH
BOOM
I THINK I CAN WORK WITH THIS!
WHAT IS GOING ON IN THERE?
YOU LOOK REALLY GUILTY, ASHA.
OKAY. FINE. LAST NIGHT I MADE A WISH...ON A STAR...
WHAT ARE YOU? FIVE?
NO, LISTEN! AND THE STAR ANSWERED.
COME WITH ME...
YOUR WINGS CAN'T FLY, BUT YOUR VOICE CAN!
WOW, I HAVE REALLY BEEN UNDERESTIMATING ANIMALS.
CLUCK
AM I DREAMING?
CLUCK
CLUCK
THAT'S A REAL STAR?
THIS IS GOING TO END VERY BADLY. OUR KING IS THE ONLY ONE AUTHORIZED TO GRANT WISHES!
DOES STAR GRANT WISHES?
NO, BUT IT DOES SEEM TO WANT TO HELP ME PURSUE MINE.
PLEASE, MAGNIFICO CAN'T KNOW ABOUT STAR. I PROMISE YOU MY WISH WON'T HARM OR AFFECT ANY OF YOU OR ROSAS.

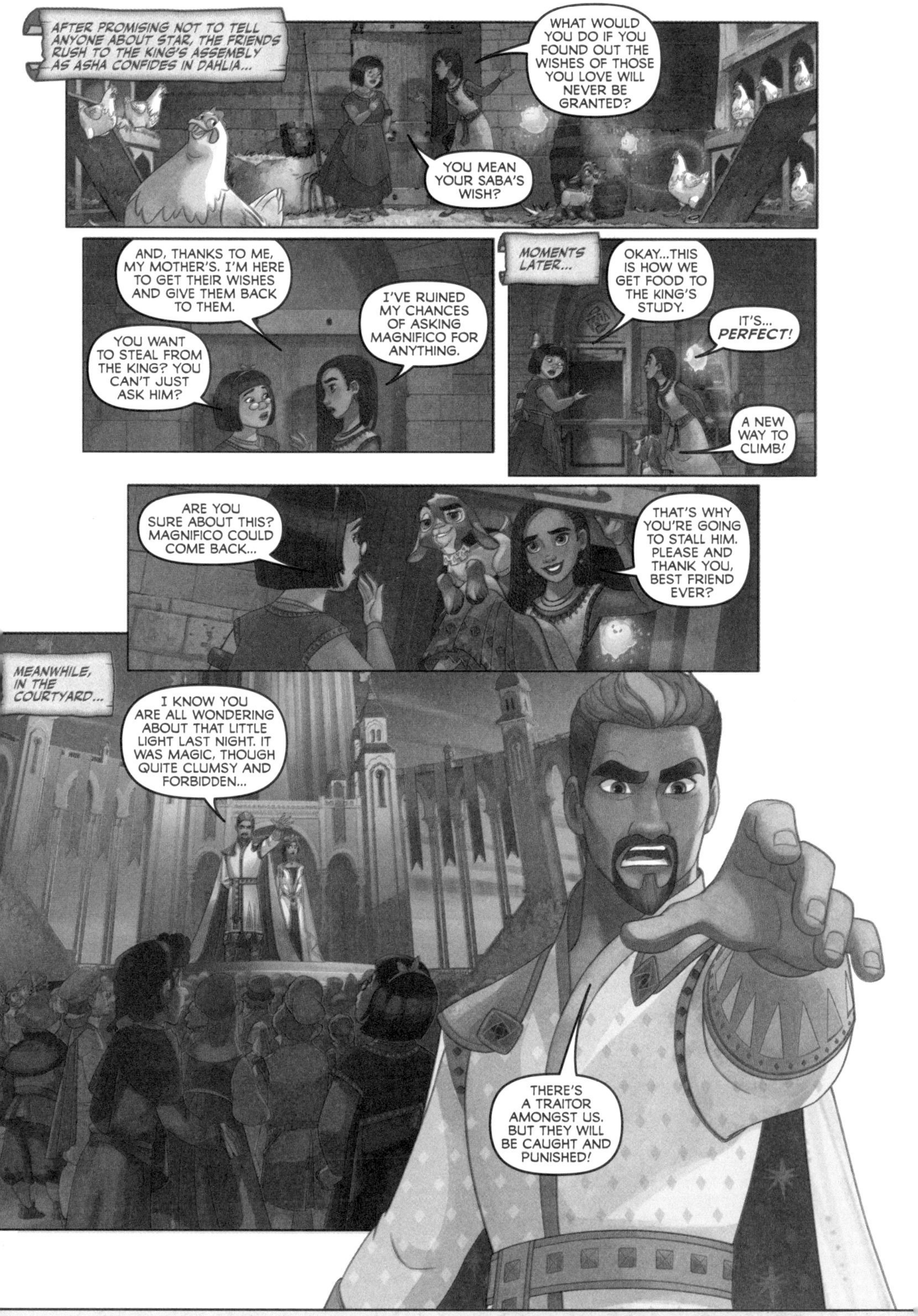
AFTER PROMISING NOT TO TELL ANYONE ABOUT STAR, THE FRIENDS RUSH TO THE KING'S ASSEMBLY AS ASHA CONFIDES IN DAHLIA...
WHAT WOULD YOU DO IF YOU FOUND OUT THE WISHES OF THOSE YOU LOVE WILL NEVER BE GRANTED?
YOU MEAN YOUR SABA'S WISH?
AND, THANKS TO ME, MY MOTHER'S. I'M HERE TO GET THEIR WISHES AND GIVE THEM BACK TO THEM.
YOU WANT TO STEAL FROM THE KING? YOU CAN'T JUST ASK HIM?
I'VE RUINED MY CHANCES OF ASKING MAGNIFICO FOR ANYTHING.
MOMENTS LATER...
OKAY...THIS IS HOW WE GET FOOD TO THE KING'S STUDY.
IT'S... PERFECT!
A NEW WAY TO CLIMB!
ARE YOU SURE ABOUT THIS? MAGNIFICO COULD COME BACK...
THAT'S WHY YOU'RE GOING TO STALL HIM. PLEASE AND THANK YOU, BEST FRIEND EVER?
MEANWHILE, IN THE COURTYARD...
I KNOW YOU ARE ALL WONDERING ABOUT THAT LITTLE LIGHT LAST NIGHT. IT WAS MAGIC, THOUGH QUITE CLUMSY AND FORBIDDEN...
THERE'S A TRAITOR AMONGST US. BUT THEY WILL BE CAUGHT AND PUNISHED!

ANY INFORMATION WILL BE HANDSOMELY REWARDED!

YOUR MAJESTY, WAIT! WHAT KIND OF INFORMATION WOULD BE MORE USEFUL? PHILOSOPHICAL? METAPHORICAL?

MEANWHILE, ASHA, STAR, AND VALENTINO ENTER THE WISH CHAMBER...

THE HUMAN IMAGINATION REALLY IS SECOND TO NONE BUT GOAT'S.

OH, HOW ARE WE SUPPOSED TO FIND MY FAMILY'S WISHES?

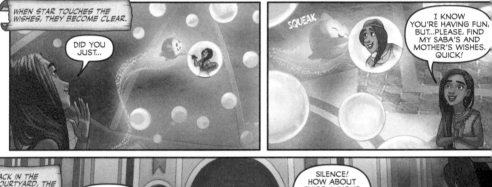

WHEN STAR TOUCHES THE WISHES, THEY BECOME CLEAR.

DID YOU JUST...

SQUEAK

I KNOW YOU'RE HAVING FUN, BUT...PLEASE, FIND MY SABA'S AND MOTHER'S WISHES. QUICK!

BACK IN THE COURTYARD, THE CROWD IS ALL WHIPPED UP...

YOU KNOW WHAT WOULD COMFORT US? ANOTHER WISH CEREMONY!

PLEASE, YOUR MAJESTY!

SILENCE! HOW ABOUT THIS? ANYONE WHO IDENTIFIES THE TRAITOR, YOUR WISH WILL BE GRANTED!

HE'S GRANTING ANOTHER WISH? HE MUST REALLY BE WORRIED...

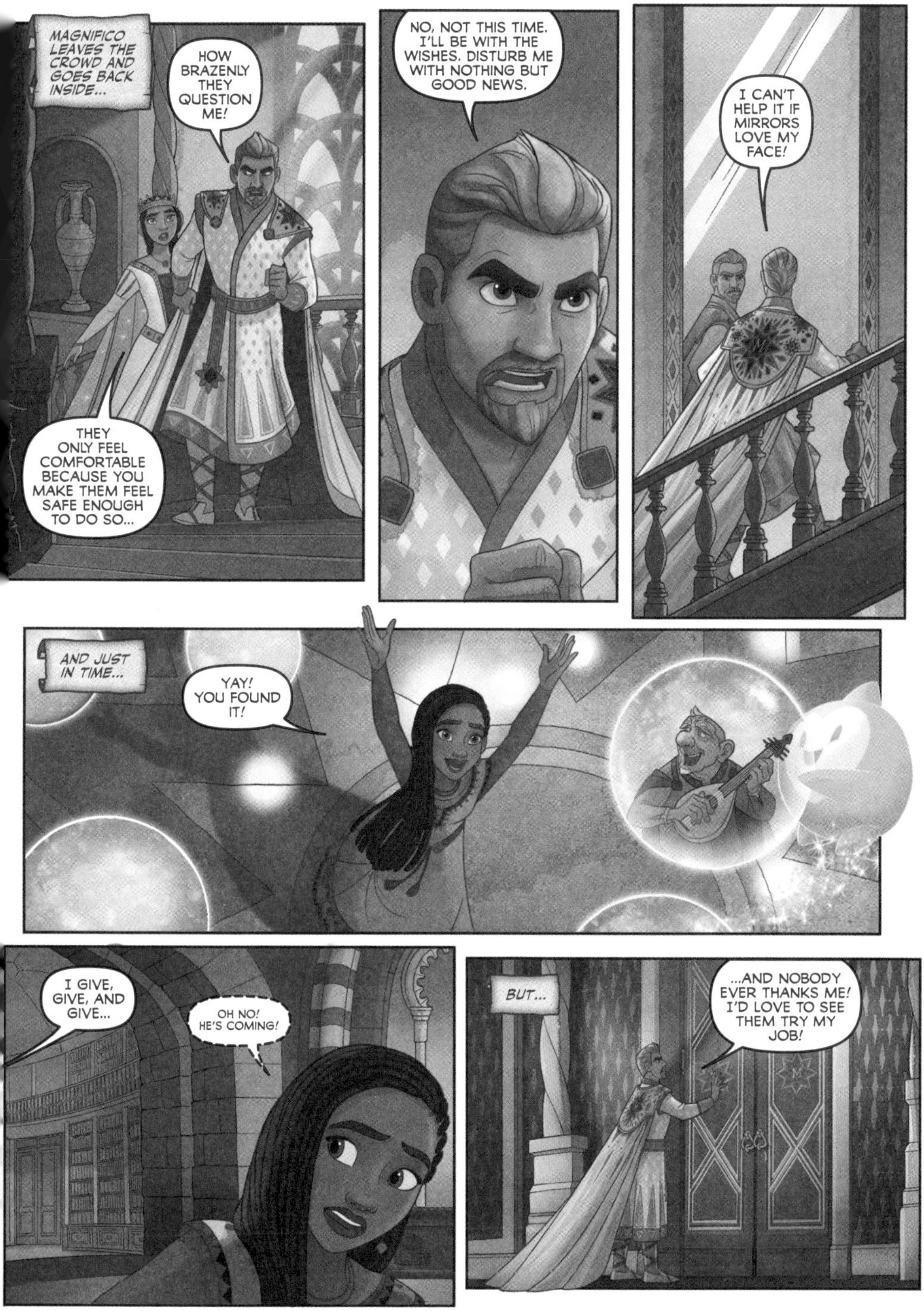
MAGNIFICO LEAVES THE CROWD AND GOES BACK INSIDE...
HOW BRAZENLY THEY QUESTION ME!
THEY ONLY FEEL COMFORTABLE BECAUSE YOU MAKE THEM FEEL SAFE ENOUGH TO DO SO...
NO, NOT THIS TIME. I'LL BE WITH THE WISHES. DISTURB ME WITH NOTHING BUT GOOD NEWS.
I CAN'T HELP IT IF MIRRORS LOVE MY FACE!
AND JUST IN TIME...
YAY! YOU FOUND IT!
I GIVE, GIVE, AND GIVE...
OH NO! HE'S COMING!
BUT...
...AND NOBODY EVER THANKS ME! I'D LOVE TO SEE THEM TRY MY JOB!

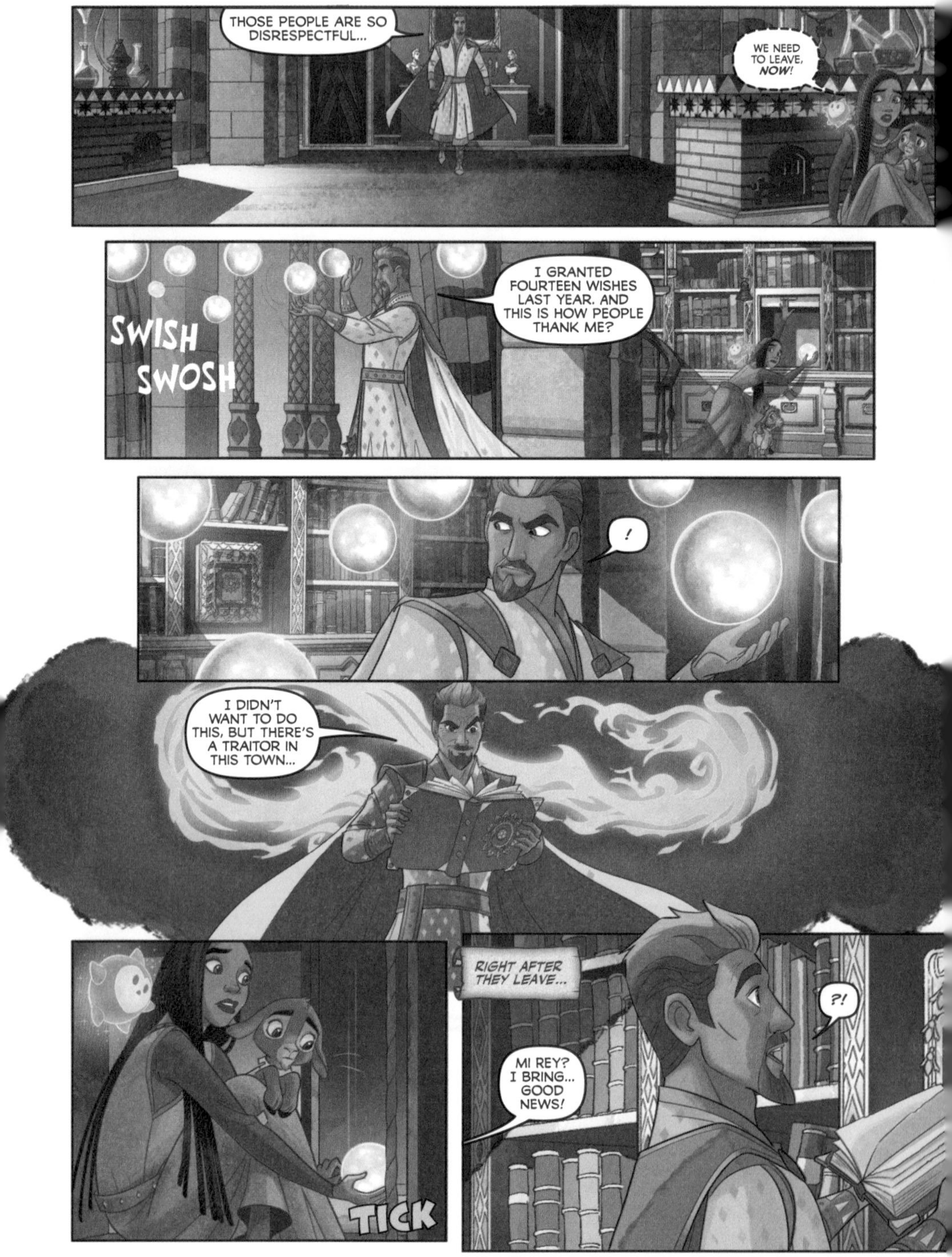
THOSE PEOPLE ARE SO DISRESPECTFUL...
WE NEED TO LEAVE, NOW!
SWISH
SWOSH
I GRANTED FOURTEEN WISHES LAST YEAR. AND THIS IS HOW PEOPLE THANK ME?
!
I DIDN'T WANT TO DO THIS, BUT THERE'S A TRAITOR IN THIS TOWN...
TICK
RIGHT AFTER THEY LEAVE...
?!
MI REY? I BRING... GOOD NEWS!

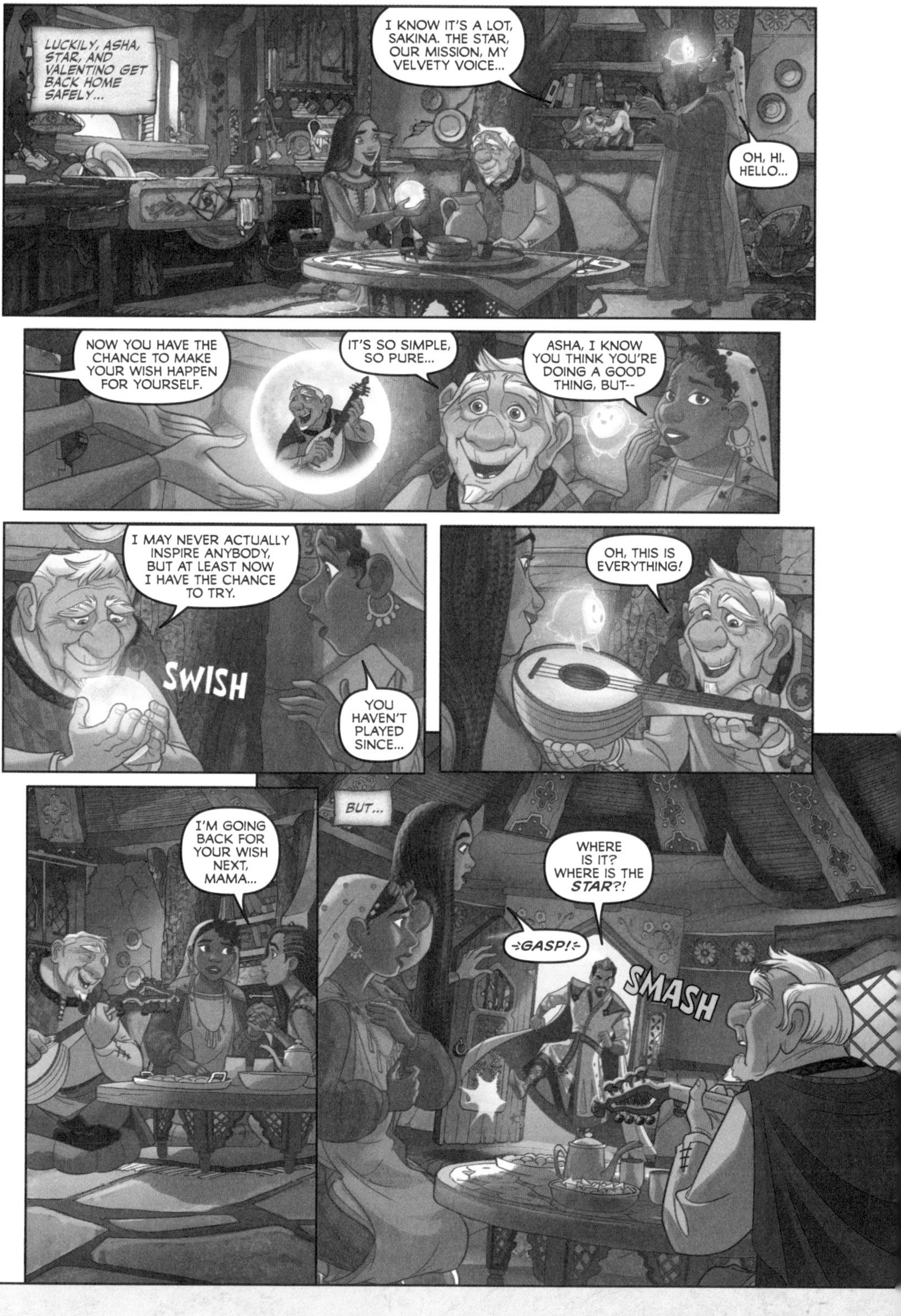

LUCKILY, ASHA, STAR, AND VALENTINO GET BACK HOME SAFELY...
I KNOW IT'S A LOT, SAKINA. THE STAR, OUR MISSION, MY VELVETY VOICE...
OH, HI. HELLO...
NOW YOU HAVE THE CHANCE TO MAKE YOUR WISH HAPPEN FOR YOURSELF.
IT'S SO SIMPLE, SO PURE...
ASHA, I KNOW YOU THINK YOU'RE DOING A GOOD THING, BUT--
I MAY NEVER ACTUALLY INSPIRE ANYBODY, BUT AT LEAST NOW I HAVE THE CHANCE TO TRY.
SWISH
YOU HAVEN'T PLAYED SINCE...
OH, THIS IS EVERYTHING!
I'M GOING BACK FOR YOUR WISH NEXT, MAMA...
BUT...
WHERE IS IT? WHERE IS THE STAR?!
GASP!
SMASH

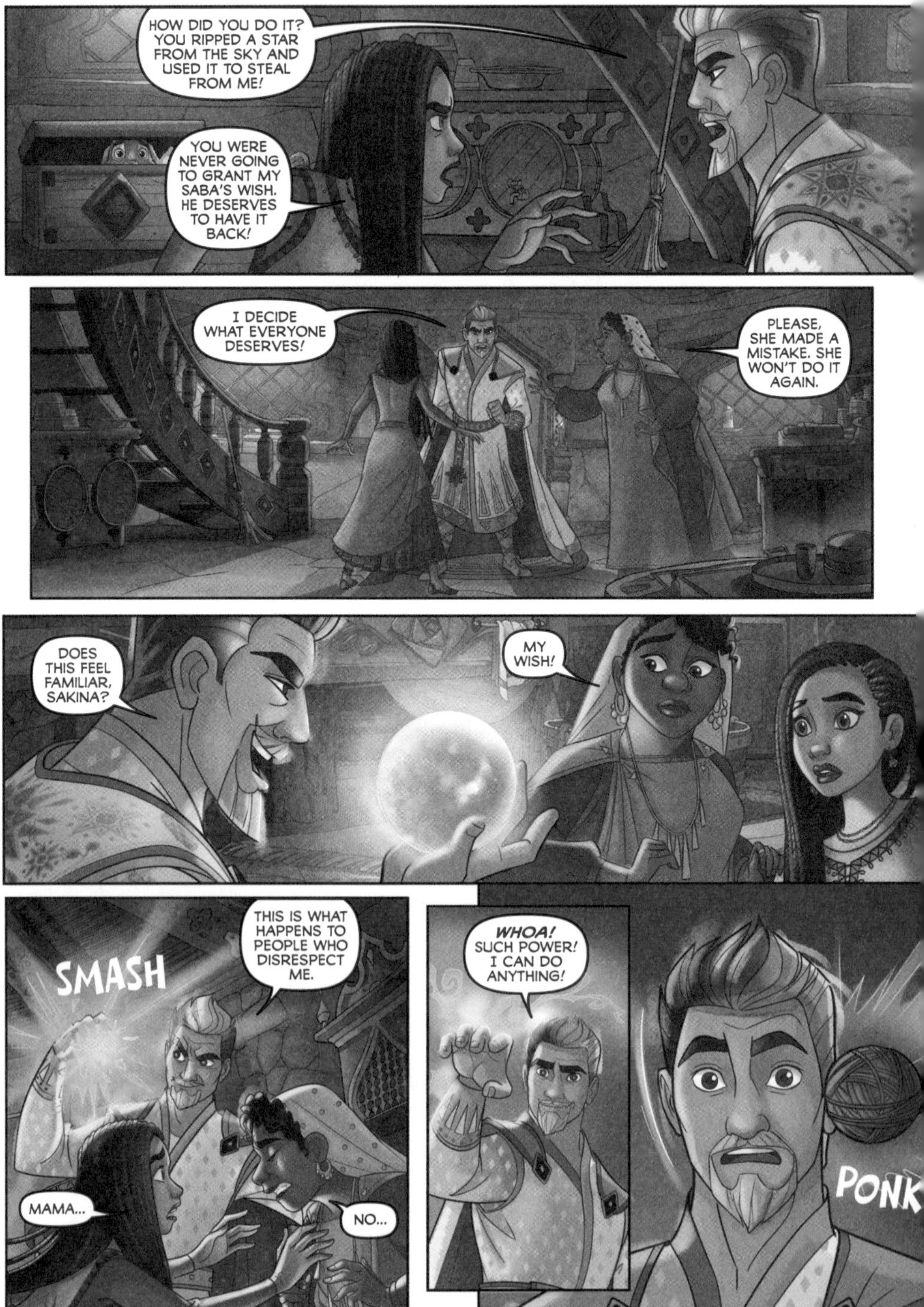
HOW DID YOU DO IT? YOU RIPPED A STAR FROM THE SKY AND USED IT TO STEAL FROM ME!
YOU WERE NEVER GOING TO GRANT MY SABA'S WISH. HE DESERVES TO HAVE IT BACK!
I DECIDE WHAT EVERYONE DESERVES!
PLEASE, SHE MADE A MISTAKE. SHE WON'T DO IT AGAIN.
DOES THIS FEEL FAMILIAR, SAKINA?
MY WISH!
SMASH
THIS IS WHAT HAPPENS TO PEOPLE WHO DISRESPECT ME.
MAMA...
NO...
WHOA! SUCH POWER! I CAN DO ANYTHING!
PONK

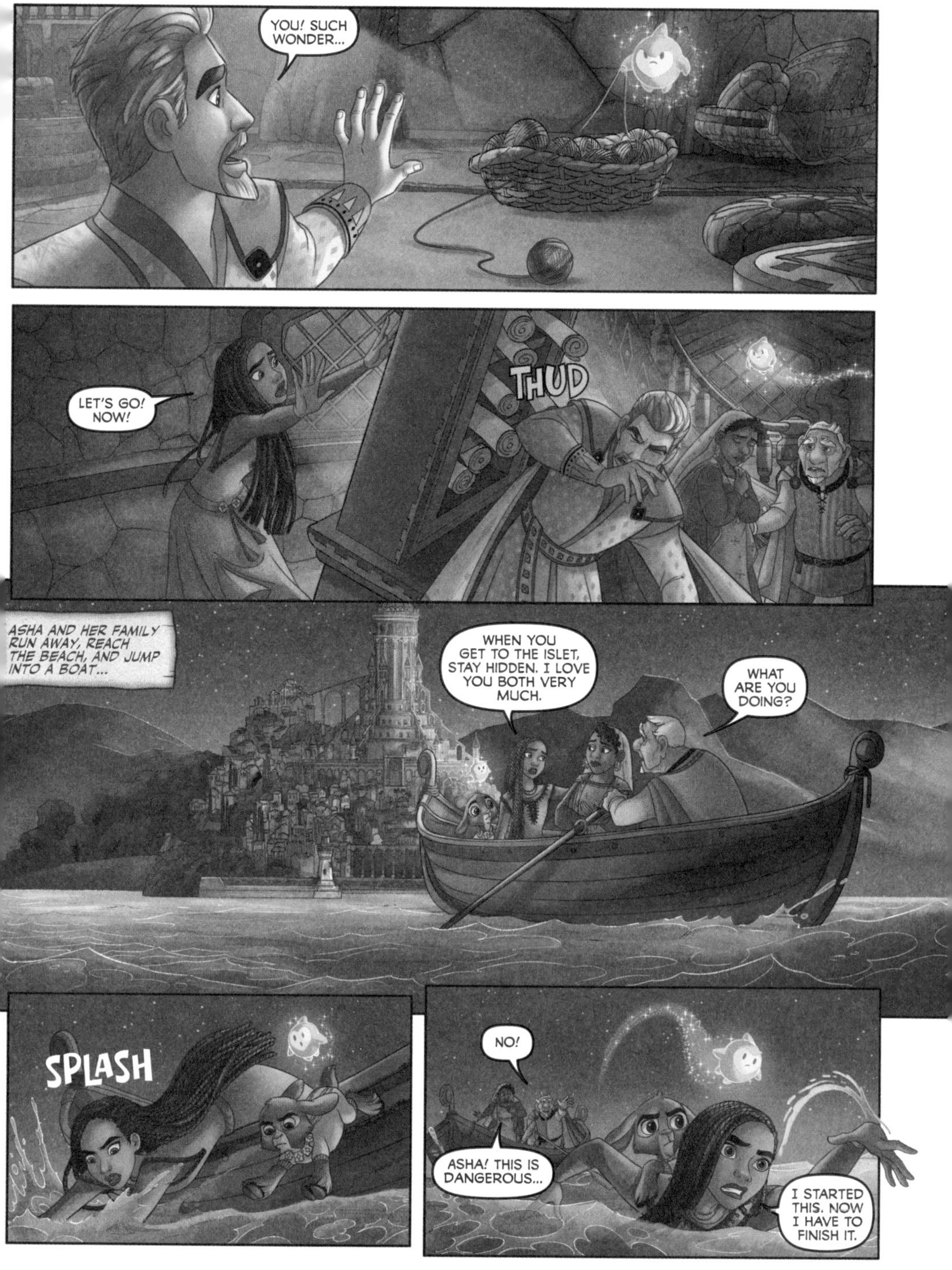
YOU! SUCH WONDER...
LET'S GO! NOW!
THUD
ASHA AND HER FAMILY RUN AWAY, REACH THE BEACH, AND JUMP INTO A BOAT...
WHEN YOU GET TO THE ISLET, STAY HIDDEN. I LOVE YOU BOTH VERY MUCH.
WHAT ARE YOU DOING?
SPLASH
NO!
ASHA! THIS IS DANGEROUS...
I STARTED THIS. NOW I HAVE TO FINISH IT.

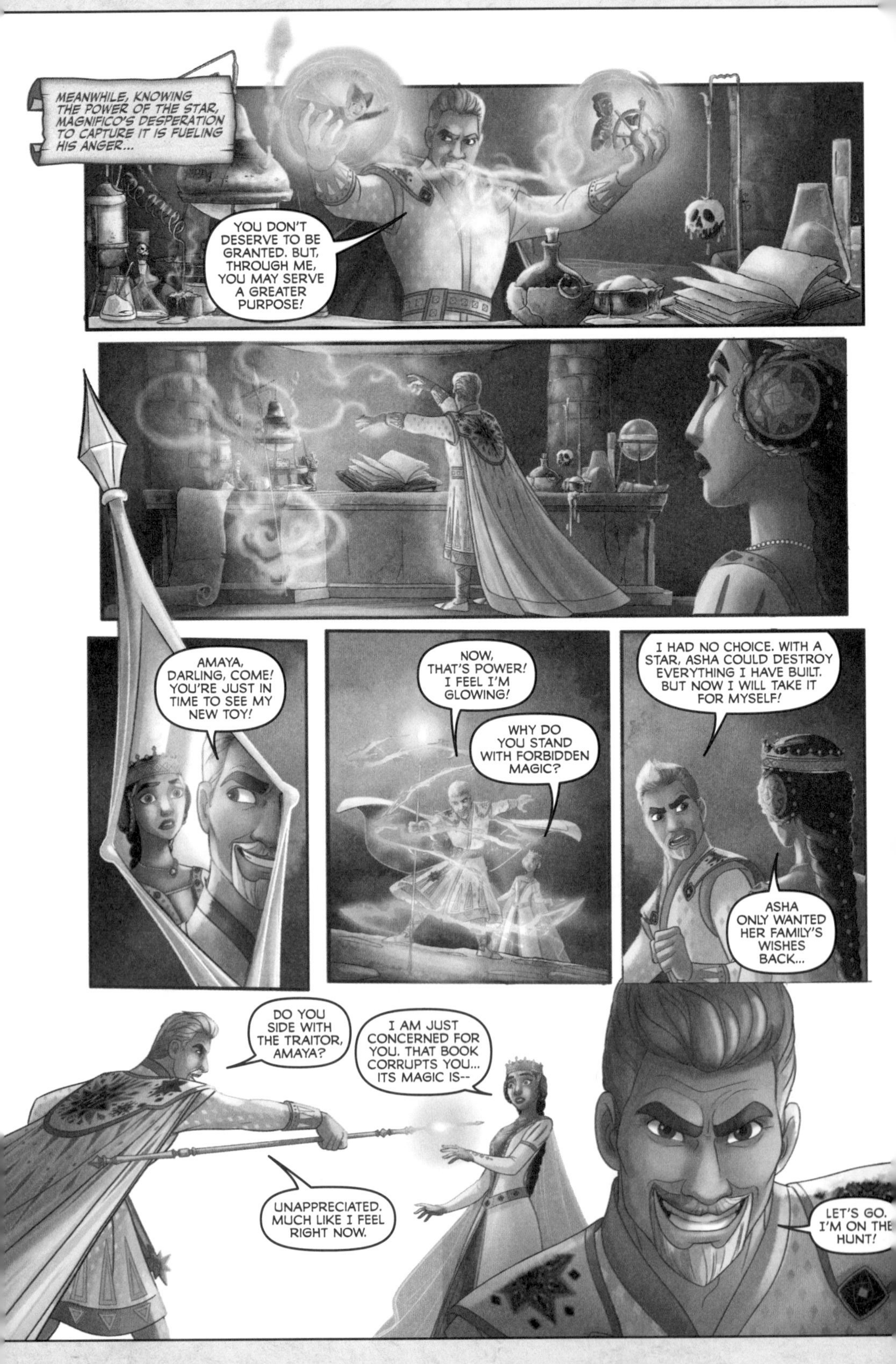
MEANWHILE, KNOWING THE POWER OF THE STAR, MAGNIFICO'S DESPERATION TO CAPTURE IT IS FUELING HIS ANGER...
YOU DON'T DESERVE TO BE GRANTED. BUT, THROUGH ME, YOU MAY SERVE A GREATER PURPOSE!
AMAYA, DARLING, COME! YOU'RE JUST IN TIME TO SEE MY NEW TOY!
NOW, THAT'S POWER! I FEEL I'M GLOWING!
WHY DO YOU STAND WITH FORBIDDEN MAGIC?
I HAD NO CHOICE. WITH A STAR, ASHA COULD DESTROY EVERYTHING I HAVE BUILT. BUT NOW I WILL TAKE IT FOR MYSELF!
ASHA ONLY WANTED HER FAMILY'S WISHES BACK...
DO YOU SIDE WITH THE TRAITOR, AMAYA?
I AM JUST CONCERNED FOR YOU. THAT BOOK CORRUPTS YOU... ITS MAGIC IS--
UNAPPRECIATED. MUCH LIKE I FEEL RIGHT NOW.
LET'S GO. I'M ON THE HUNT!

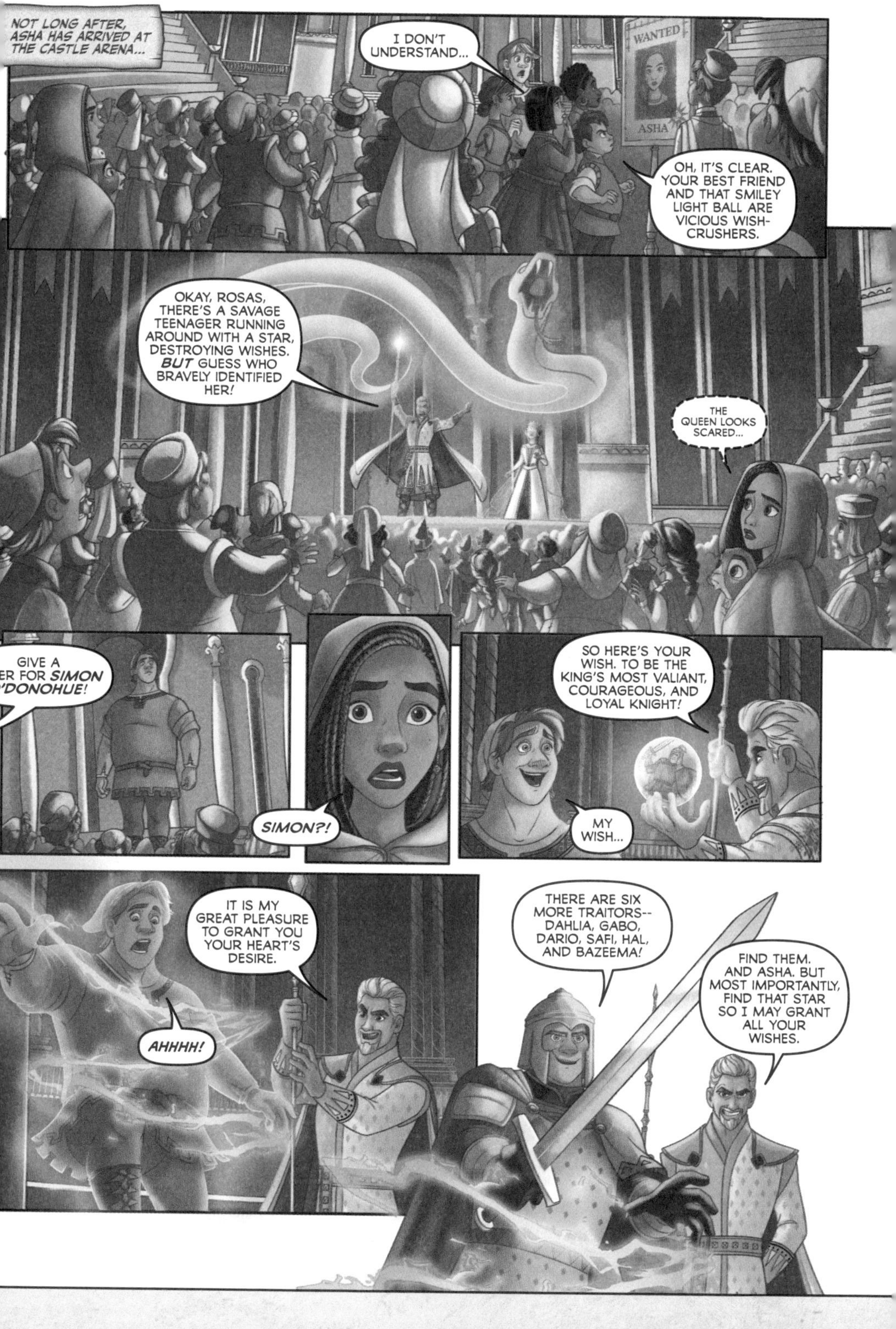
NOT LONG AFTER, ASHA HAS ARRIVED AT THE CASTLE ARENA...
I DON'T UNDERSTAND...
WANTED
ASHA
OH, IT'S CLEAR. YOUR BEST FRIEND AND THAT SMILEY LIGHT BALL ARE VICIOUS WISH-CRUSHERS.
OKAY, ROSAS, THERE'S A SAVAGE TEENAGER RUNNING AROUND WITH A STAR, DESTROYING WISHES. **BUT** GUESS WHO BRAVELY IDENTIFIED HER!
THE QUEEN LOOKS SCARED...
GIVE A ER FOR **SIMON 'DONOHUE**!
SIMON?!
SO HERE'S YOUR WISH. TO BE THE KING'S MOST VALIANT, COURAGEOUS, AND LOYAL KNIGHT!
MY WISH...
IT IS MY GREAT PLEASURE TO GRANT YOU YOUR HEART'S DESIRE.
AHHHH!
THERE ARE SIX MORE TRAITORS-- DAHLIA, GABO, DARIO, SAFI, HAL, AND BAZEEMA!
FIND THEM. AND ASHA. BUT MOST IMPORTANTLY, FIND THAT STAR SO I MAY GRANT ALL YOUR WISHES.

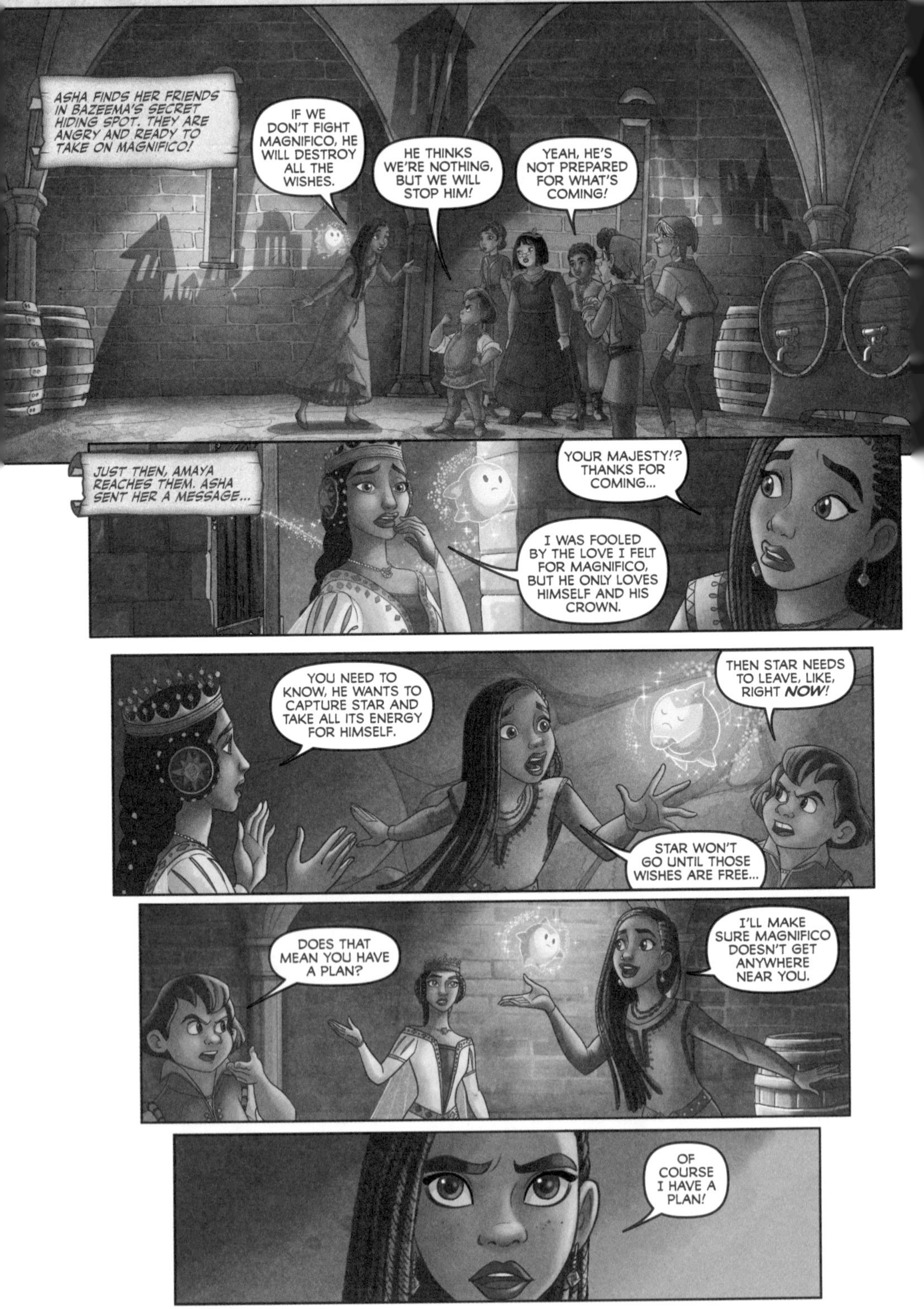
ASHA FINDS HER FRIENDS IN BAZEEMA'S SECRET HIDING SPOT. THEY ARE ANGRY AND READY TO TAKE ON MAGNIFICO!
IF WE DON'T FIGHT MAGNIFICO, HE WILL DESTROY ALL THE WISHES.
HE THINKS WE'RE NOTHING, BUT WE WILL STOP HIM!
YEAH, HE'S NOT PREPARED FOR WHAT'S COMING!
JUST THEN, AMAYA REACHES THEM. ASHA SENT HER A MESSAGE...
YOUR MAJESTY!? THANKS FOR COMING...
I WAS FOOLED BY THE LOVE I FELT FOR MAGNIFICO, BUT HE ONLY LOVES HIMSELF AND HIS CROWN.
YOU NEED TO KNOW, HE WANTS TO CAPTURE STAR AND TAKE ALL ITS ENERGY FOR HIMSELF.
THEN STAR NEEDS TO LEAVE, LIKE, RIGHT NOW!
STAR WON'T GO UNTIL THOSE WISHES ARE FREE...
DOES THAT MEAN YOU HAVE A PLAN?
I'LL MAKE SURE MAGNIFICO DOESN'T GET ANYWHERE NEAR YOU.
OF COURSE I HAVE A PLAN!

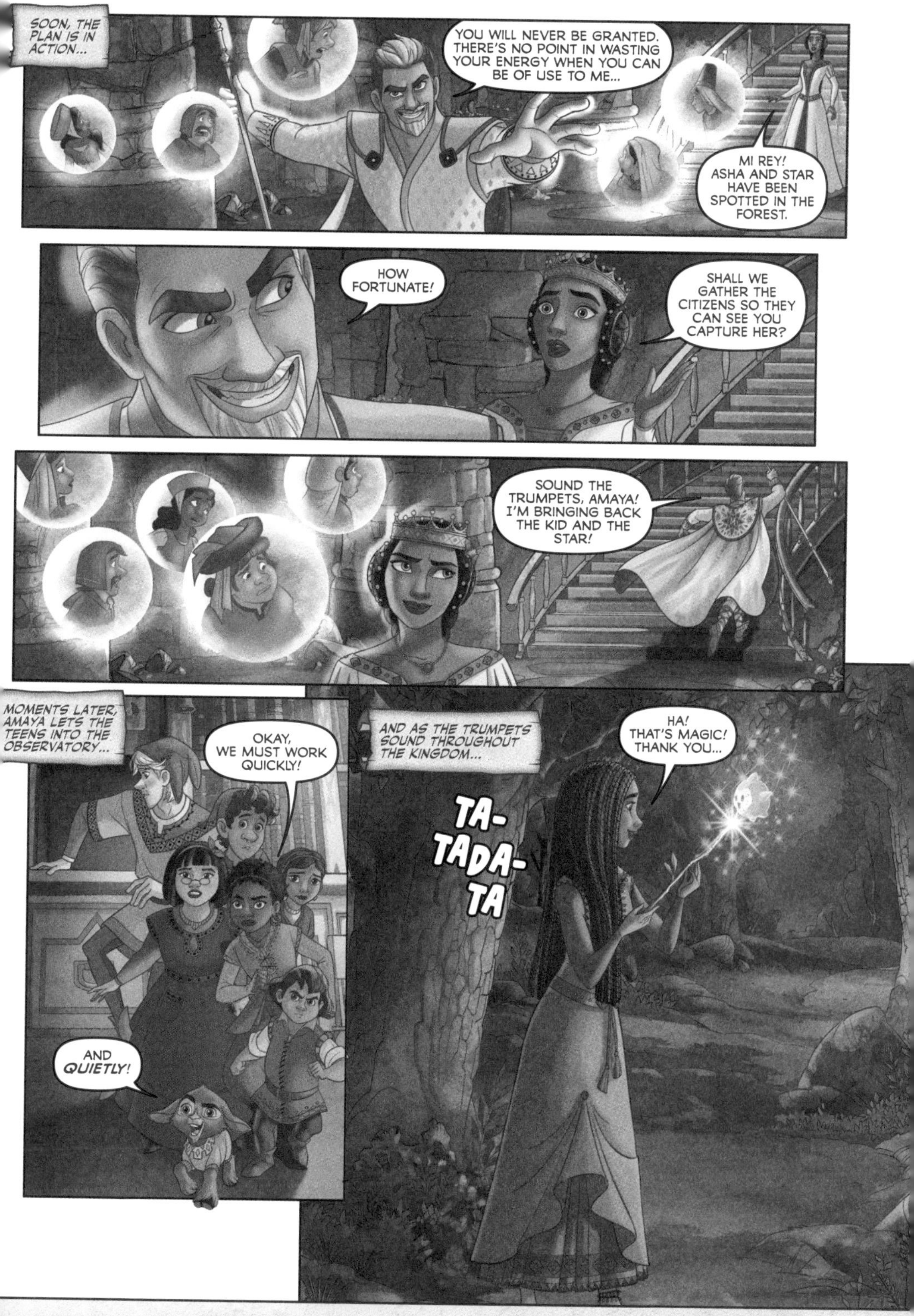
SOON, THE PLAN IS IN ACTION...
YOU WILL NEVER BE GRANTED. THERE'S NO POINT IN WASTING YOUR ENERGY WHEN YOU CAN BE OF USE TO ME...
MI REY! ASHA AND STAR HAVE BEEN SPOTTED IN THE FOREST.
HOW FORTUNATE!
SHALL WE GATHER THE CITIZENS SO THEY CAN SEE YOU CAPTURE HER?
SOUND THE TRUMPETS, AMAYA! I'M BRINGING BACK THE KID AND THE STAR!
MOMENTS LATER, AMAYA LETS THE TEENS INTO THE OBSERVATORY...
OKAY, WE MUST WORK QUICKLY!
AND QUIETLY!
AND AS THE TRUMPETS SOUND THROUGHOUT THE KINGDOM...
HA! THAT'S MAGIC! THANK YOU...
TA-TADA-TA

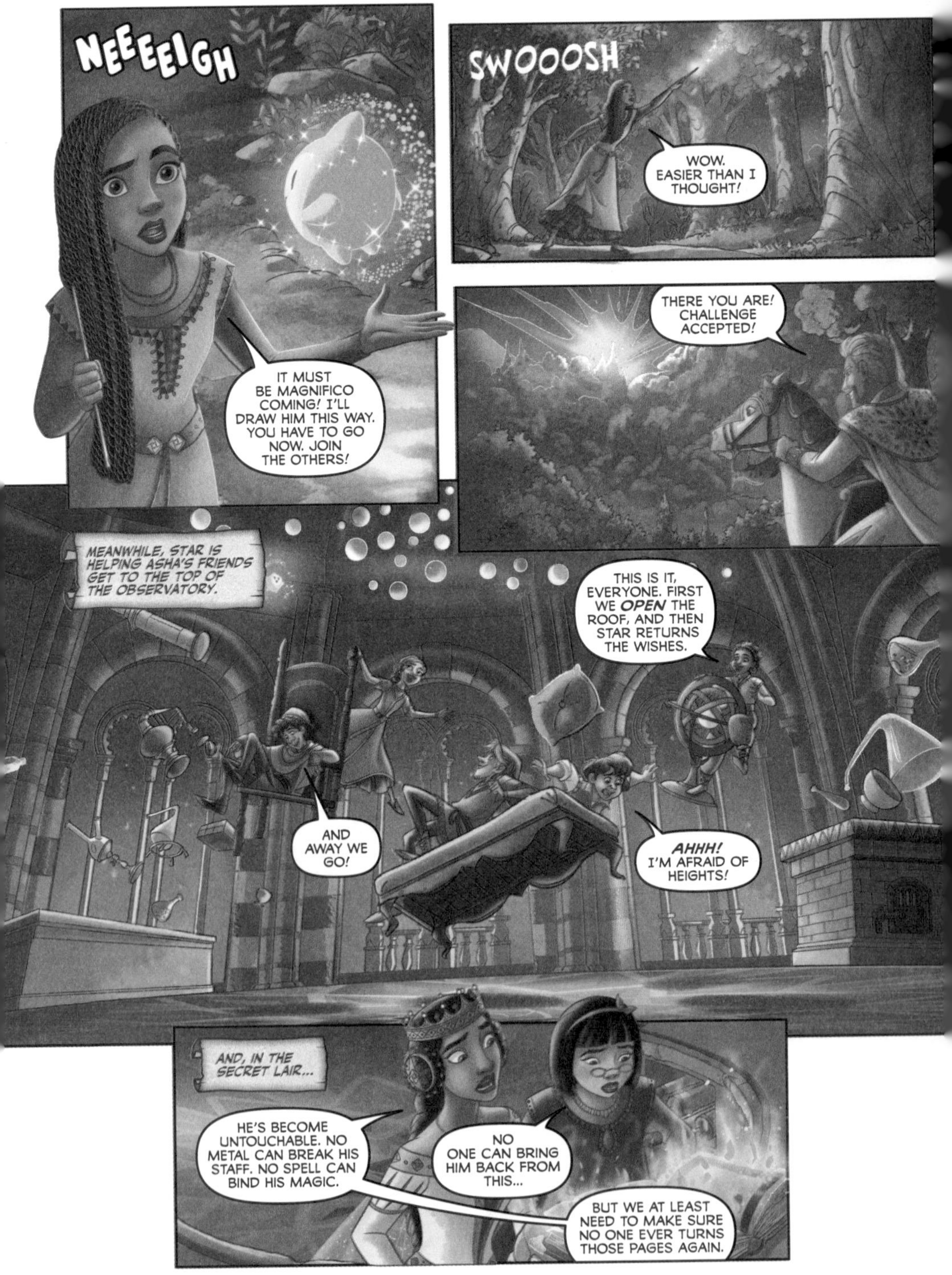
NEEEEIGH
IT MUST BE MAGNIFICO COMING! I'LL DRAW HIM THIS WAY. YOU HAVE TO GO NOW. JOIN THE OTHERS!
SWOOOSH
WOW. EASIER THAN I THOUGHT!
THERE YOU ARE! CHALLENGE ACCEPTED!
MEANWHILE, STAR IS HELPING ASHA'S FRIENDS GET TO THE TOP OF THE OBSERVATORY.
THIS IS IT, EVERYONE. FIRST WE OPEN THE ROOF, AND THEN STAR RETURNS THE WISHES.
AND AWAY WE GO!
AHHH! I'M AFRAID OF HEIGHTS!
AND, IN THE SECRET LAIR...
HE'S BECOME UNTOUCHABLE. NO METAL CAN BREAK HIS STAFF. NO SPELL CAN BIND HIS MAGIC.
NO ONE CAN BRING HIM BACK FROM THIS...
BUT WE AT LEAST NEED TO MAKE SURE NO ONE EVER TURNS THOSE PAGES AGAIN.

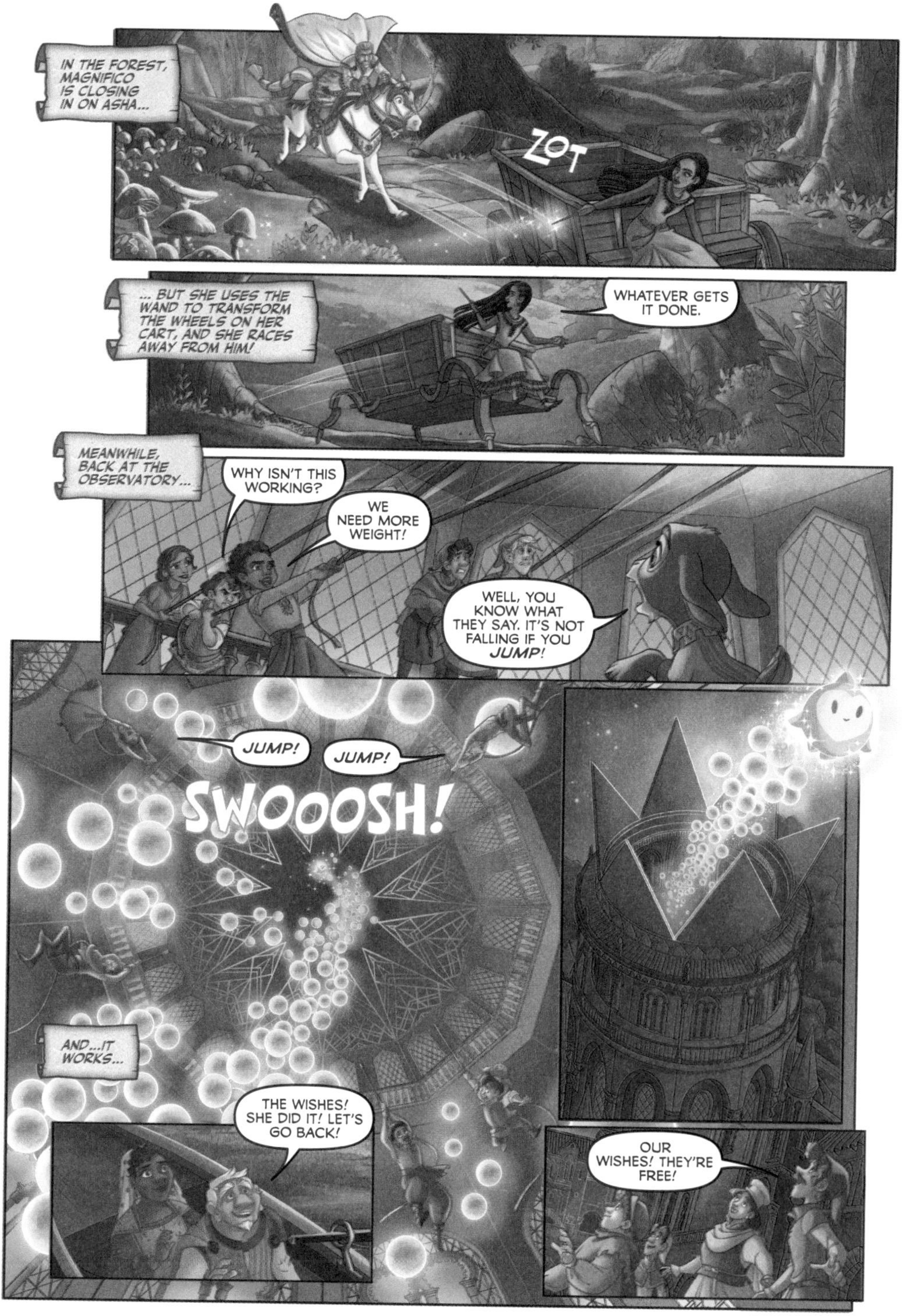
IN THE FOREST, MAGNIFICO IS CLOSING IN ON ASHA...
ZOT
... BUT SHE USES THE WAND TO TRANSFORM THE WHEELS ON HER CART, AND SHE RACES AWAY FROM HIM!
WHATEVER GETS IT DONE.
MEANWHILE, BACK AT THE OBSERVATORY...
WHY ISN'T THIS WORKING?
WE NEED MORE WEIGHT!
WELL, YOU KNOW WHAT THEY SAY. IT'S NOT FALLING IF YOU *JUMP!*
JUMP!
JUMP!
SWOOOSH!
AND...IT WORKS...
THE WISHES! SHE DID IT! LET'S GO BACK!
OUR WISHES! THEY'RE FREE!

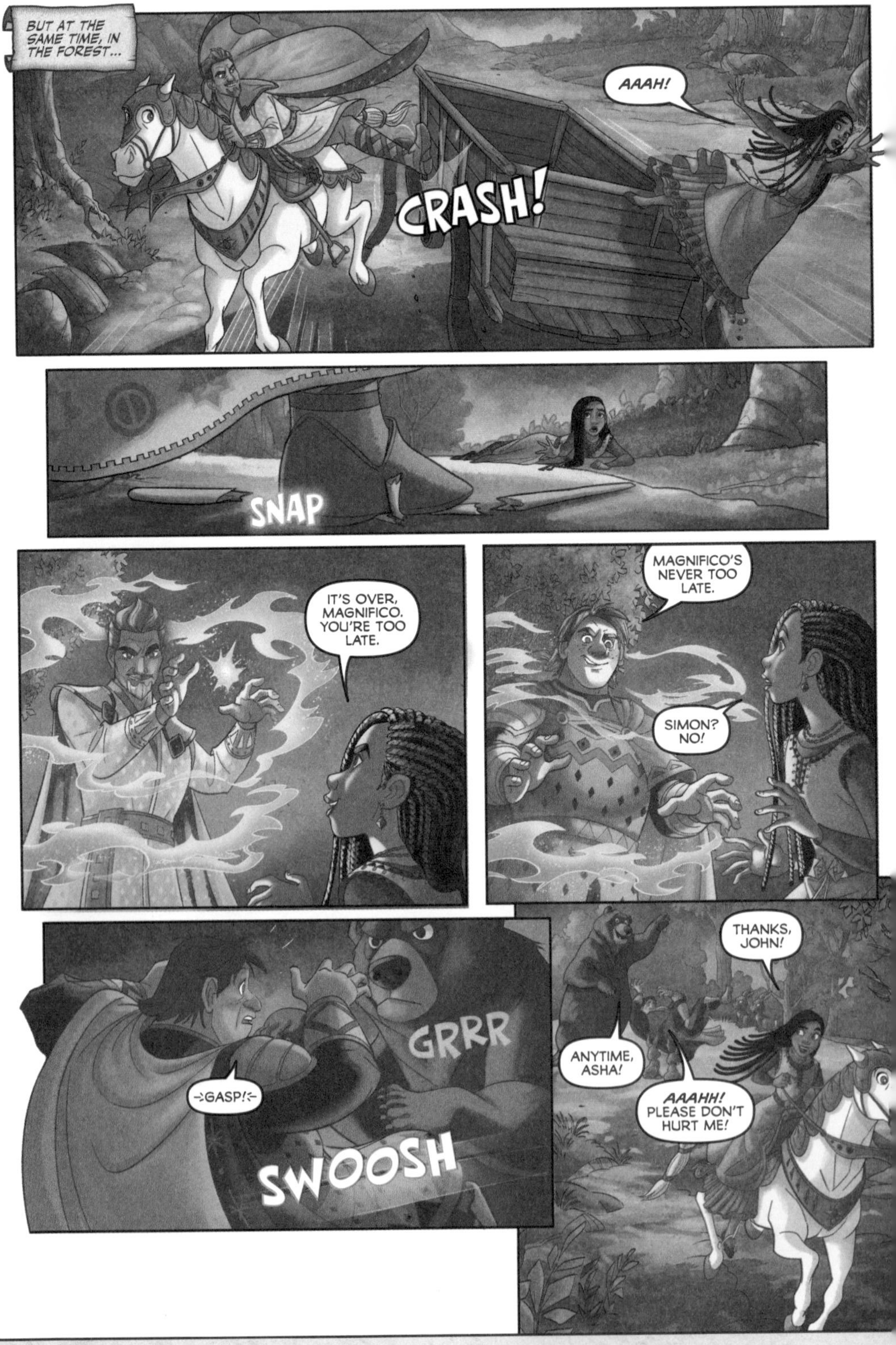
BUT AT THE SAME TIME, IN THE FOREST...
AAAH!
CRASH!
SNAP
IT'S OVER, MAGNIFICO. YOU'RE TOO LATE.
MAGNIFICO'S NEVER TOO LATE.
SIMON? NO!
GRRR
GASP!
SWOOSH
THANKS, JOHN!
ANYTIME, ASHA!
AAAHH! PLEASE DON'T HURT ME!

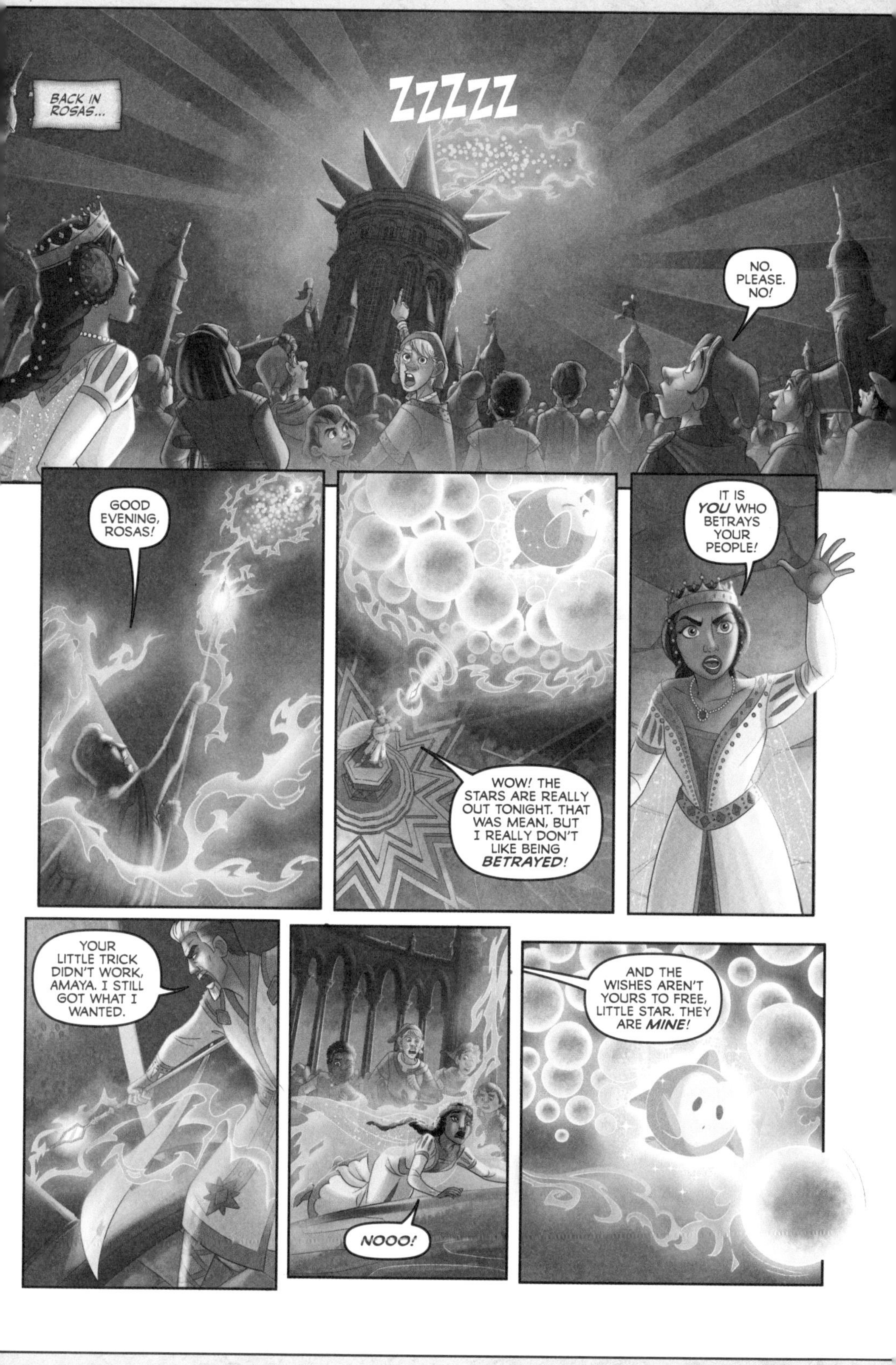
BACK IN ROSAS...
ZZZZZ
NO. PLEASE. NO!
GOOD EVENING, ROSAS!
WOW! THE STARS ARE REALLY OUT TONIGHT. THAT WAS MEAN, BUT I REALLY DON'T LIKE BEING BETRAYED!
IT IS YOU WHO BETRAYS YOUR PEOPLE!
YOUR LITTLE TRICK DIDN'T WORK, AMAYA. I STILL GOT WHAT I WANTED.
NOOO!
AND THE WISHES AREN'T YOURS TO FREE, LITTLE STAR. THEY ARE MINE!

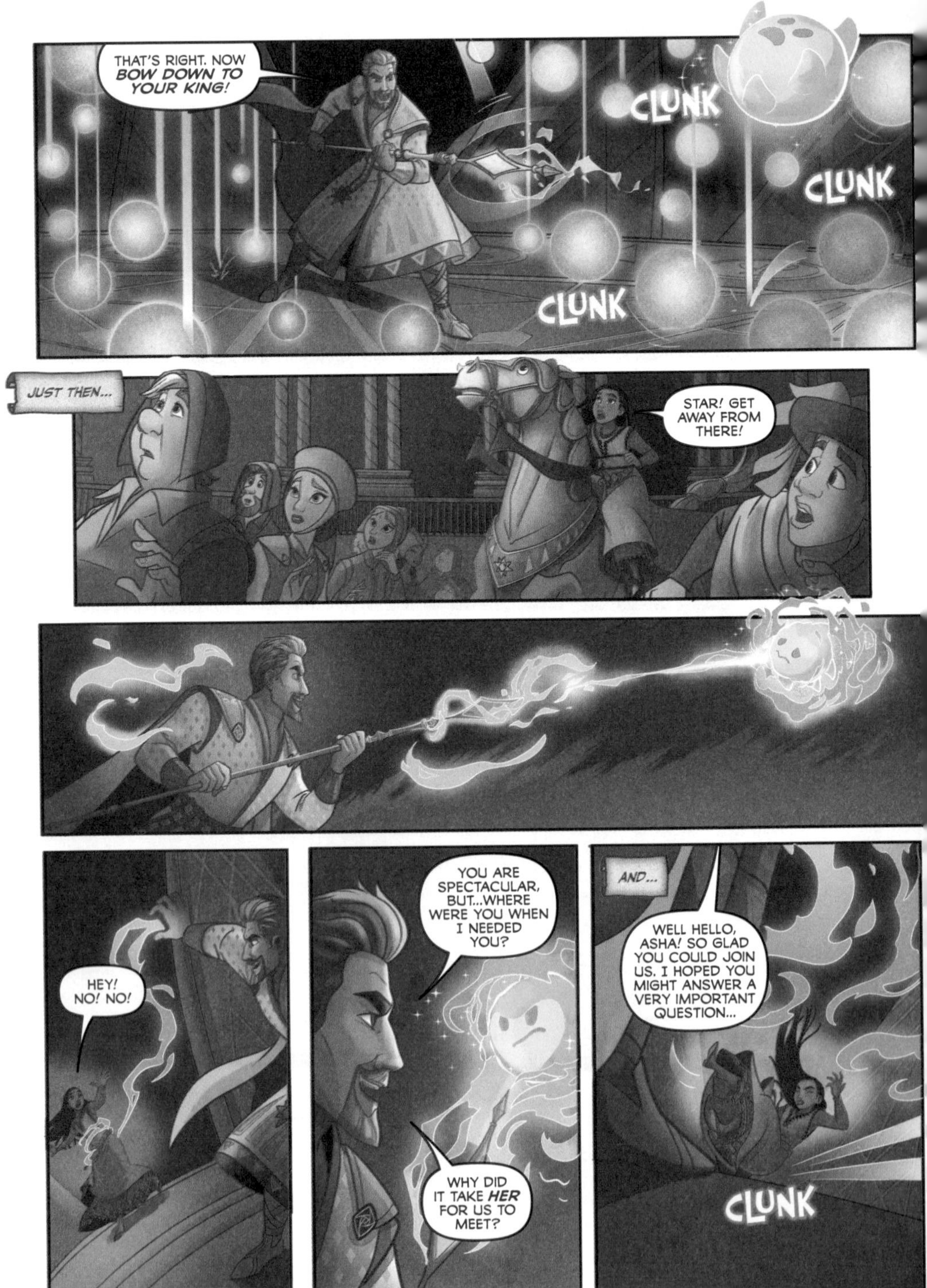

THAT'S RIGHT. NOW *BOW DOWN TO YOUR KING!*
CLUNK
CLUNK
CLUNK
JUST THEN...
STAR! GET AWAY FROM THERE!
HEY! NO! NO!
YOU ARE SPECTACULAR, BUT...WHERE WERE YOU WHEN I NEEDED YOU?
WHY DID IT TAKE *HER* FOR US TO MEET?
AND...
WELL HELLO, ASHA! SO GLAD YOU COULD JOIN US. I HOPED YOU MIGHT ANSWER A VERY IMPORTANT QUESTION...
CLUNK

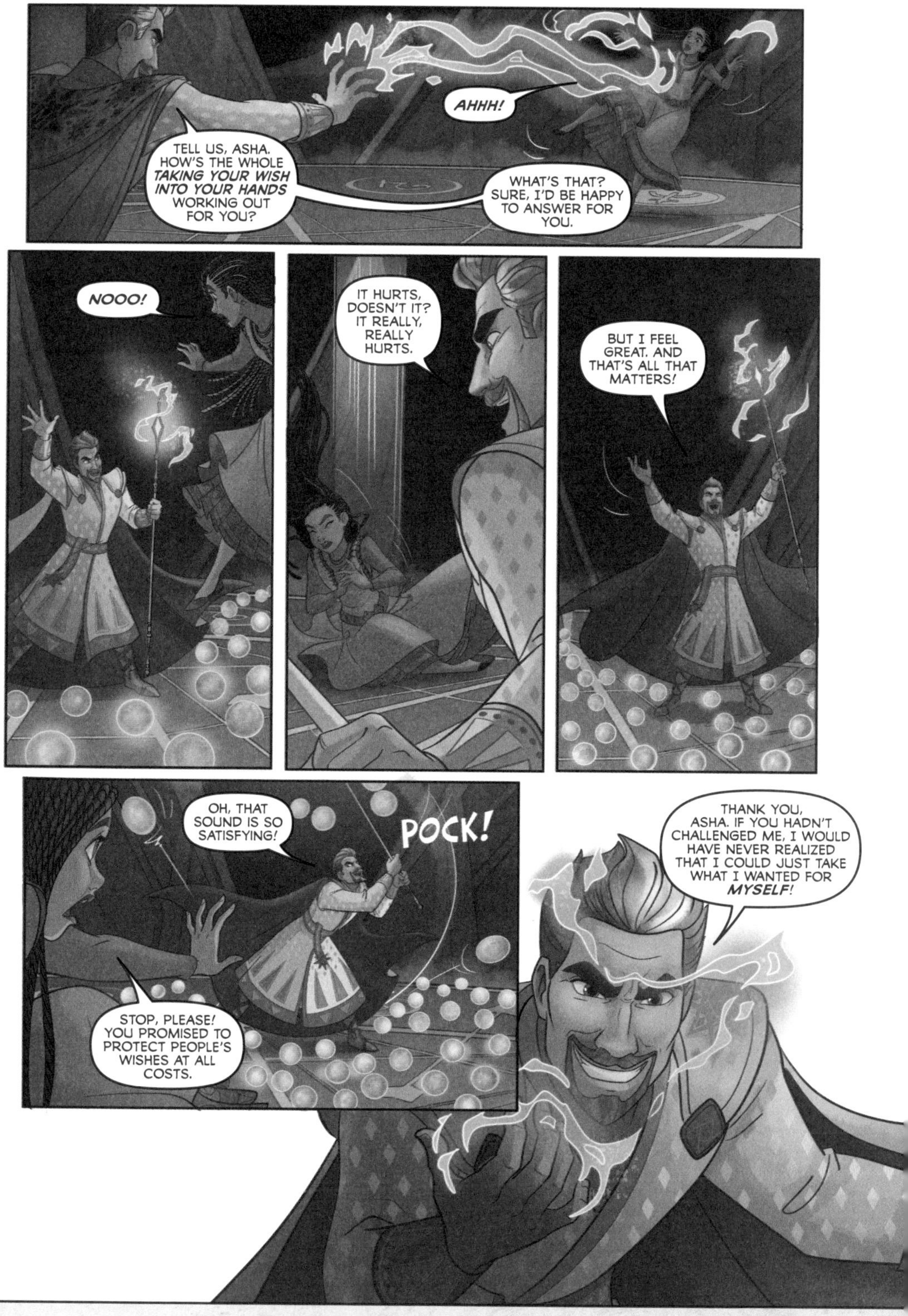
AHHH!
TELL US, ASHA. HOW'S THE WHOLE *TAKING YOUR WISH INTO YOUR HANDS* WORKING OUT FOR YOU?
WHAT'S THAT? SURE, I'D BE HAPPY TO ANSWER FOR YOU.
NOOO!
IT HURTS, DOESN'T IT? IT REALLY, REALLY HURTS.
BUT I FEEL GREAT. AND THAT'S ALL THAT MATTERS!
OH, THAT SOUND IS SO SATISFYING!
POCK!
STOP, PLEASE! YOU PROMISED TO PROTECT PEOPLE'S WISHES AT ALL COSTS.
THANK YOU, ASHA. IF YOU HADN'T CHALLENGED ME, I WOULD HAVE NEVER REALIZED THAT I COULD JUST TAKE WHAT I WANTED FOR ***MYSELF***!

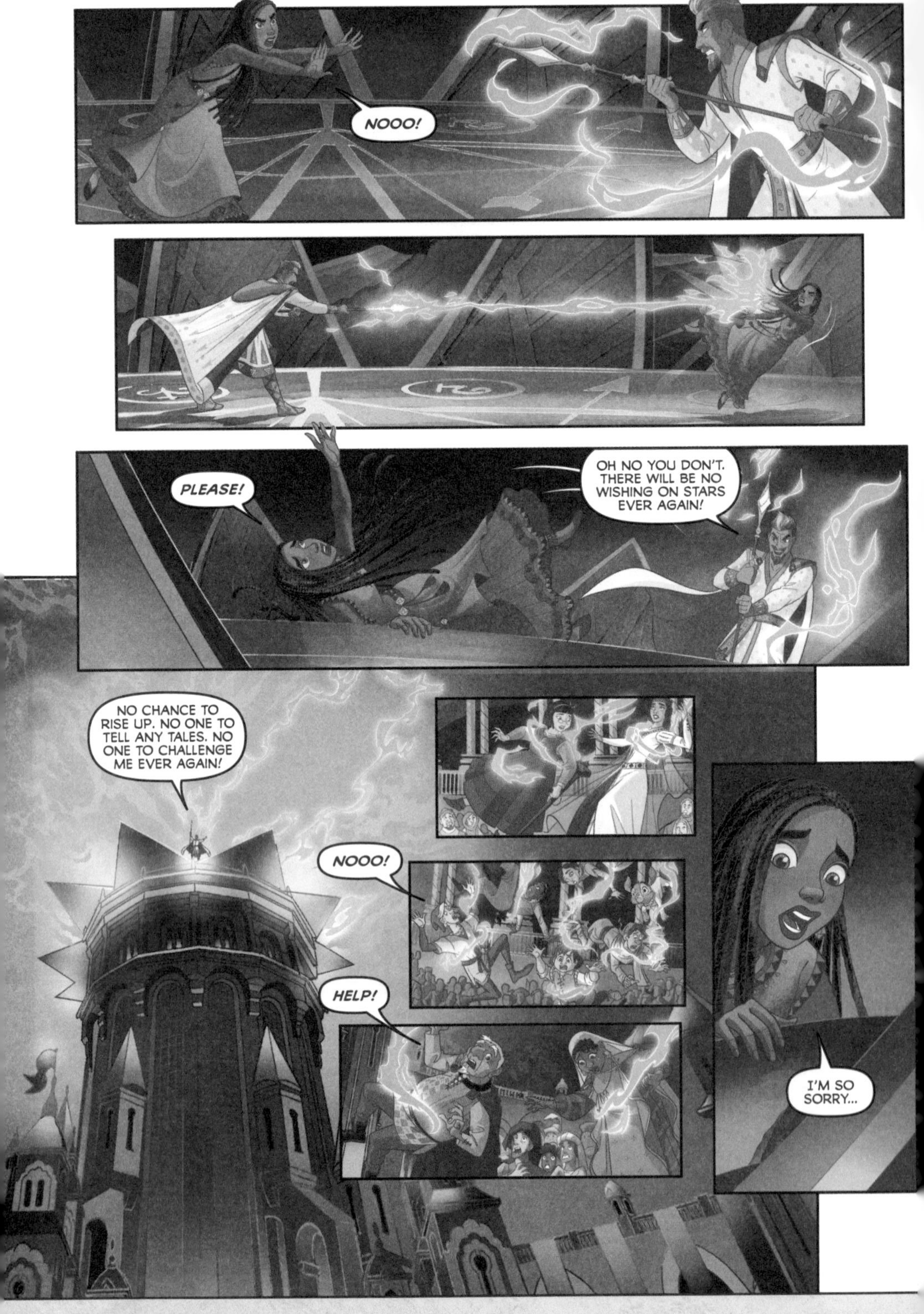
NOOO!
PLEASE!
OH NO YOU DON'T. THERE WILL BE NO WISHING ON STARS EVER AGAIN!
NO CHANCE TO RISE UP. NO ONE TO TELL ANY TALES. NO ONE TO CHALLENGE ME EVER AGAIN!
NOOO!
HELP!
I'M SO SORRY...

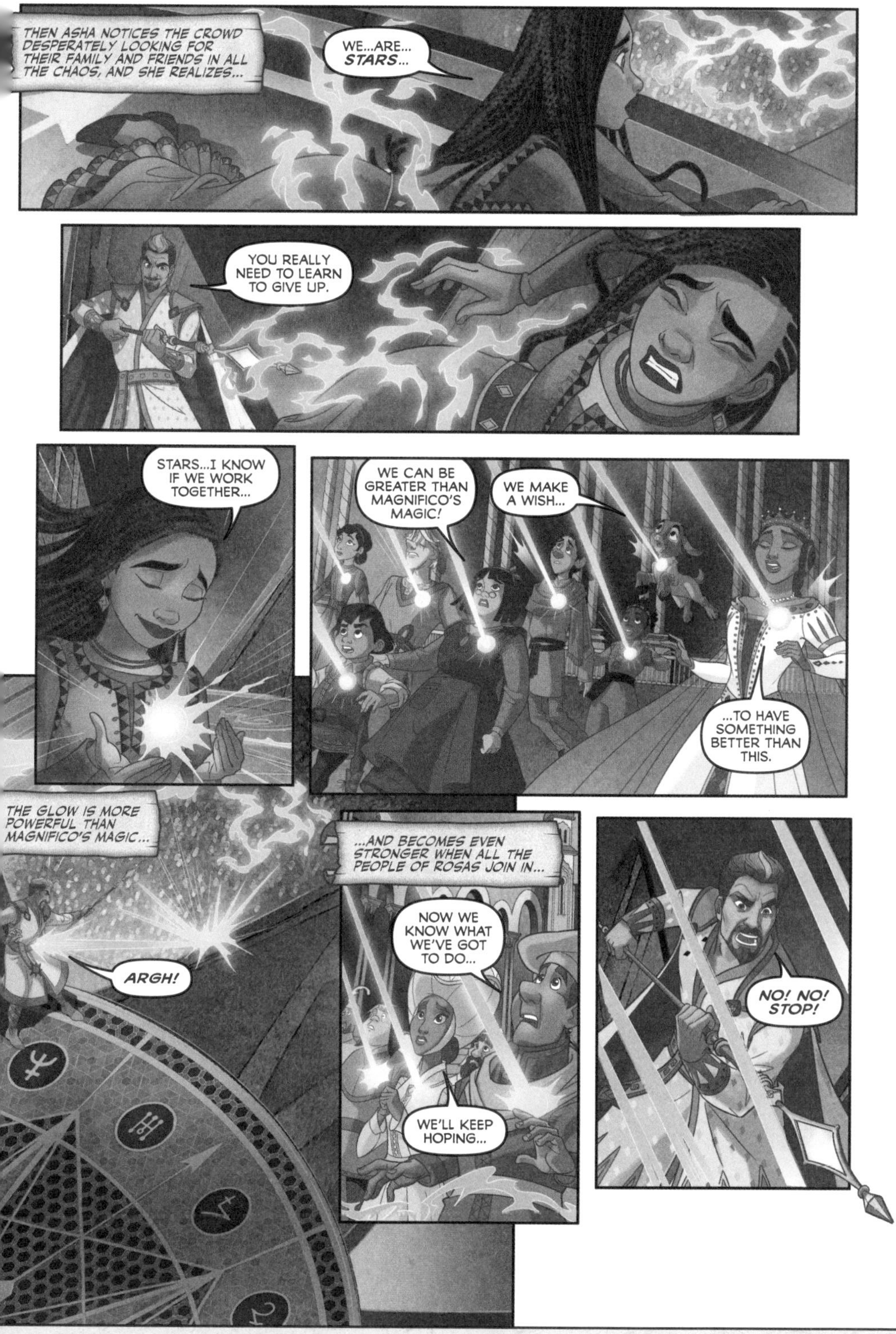
THEN ASHA NOTICES THE CROWD DESPERATELY LOOKING FOR THEIR FAMILY AND FRIENDS IN ALL THE CHAOS, AND SHE REALIZES...
WE...ARE... STARS...
YOU REALLY NEED TO LEARN TO GIVE UP.
STARS...I KNOW IF WE WORK TOGETHER...
WE CAN BE GREATER THAN MAGNIFICO'S MAGIC!
WE MAKE A WISH...
...TO HAVE SOMETHING BETTER THAN THIS.
THE GLOW IS MORE POWERFUL THAN MAGNIFICO'S MAGIC...
ARGH!
...AND BECOMES EVEN STRONGER WHEN ALL THE PEOPLE OF ROSAS JOIN IN...
NOW WE KNOW WHAT WE'VE GOT TO DO...
WE'LL KEEP HOPING...
NO! NO! STOP!

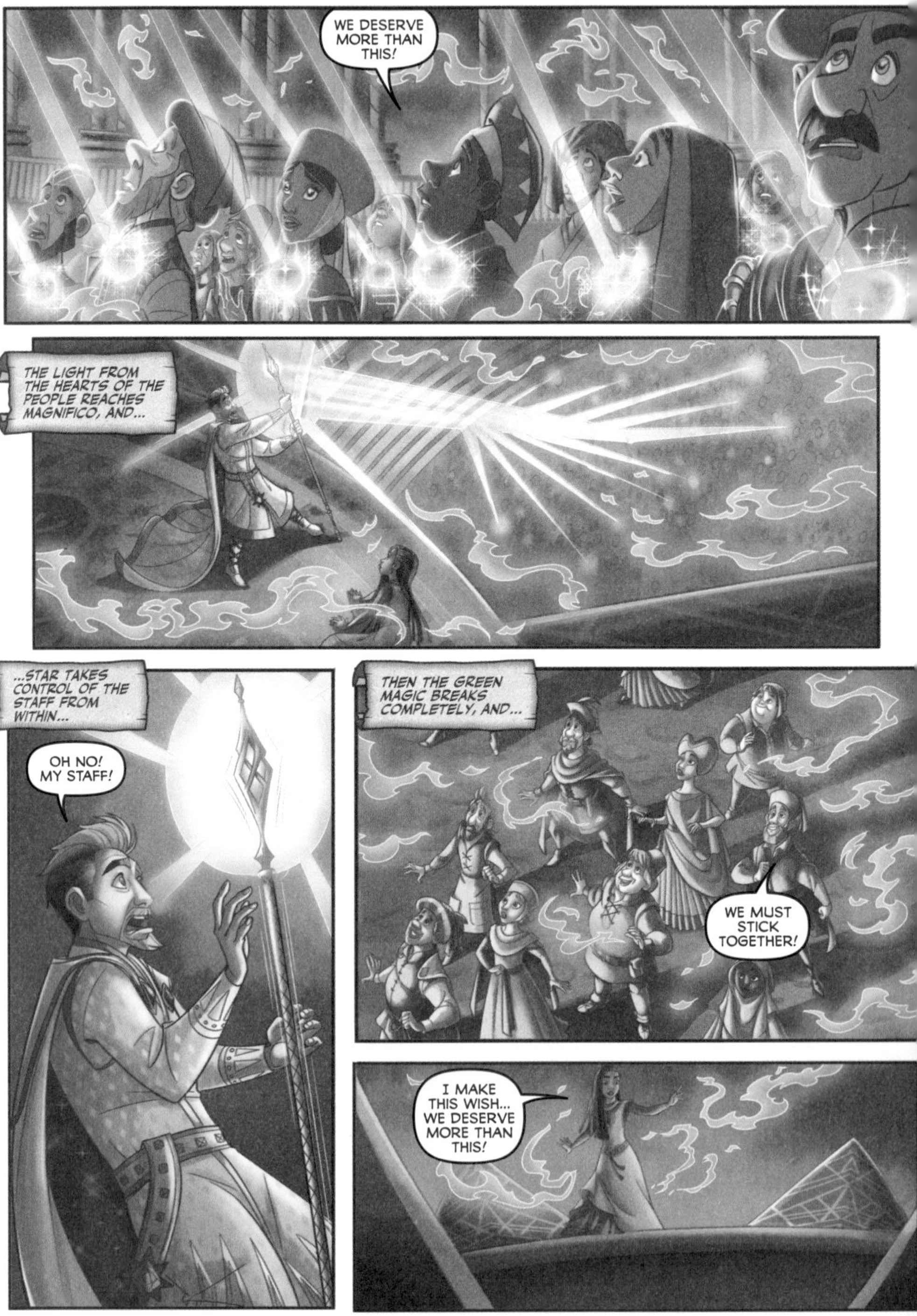
WE DESERVE MORE THAN THIS!
THE LIGHT FROM THE HEARTS OF THE PEOPLE REACHES MAGNIFICO, AND...
...STAR TAKES CONTROL OF THE STAFF FROM WITHIN...
OH NO! MY STAFF!
THEN THE GREEN MAGIC BREAKS COMPLETELY, AND...
WE MUST STICK TOGETHER!
I MAKE THIS WISH... WE DESERVE MORE THAN THIS!

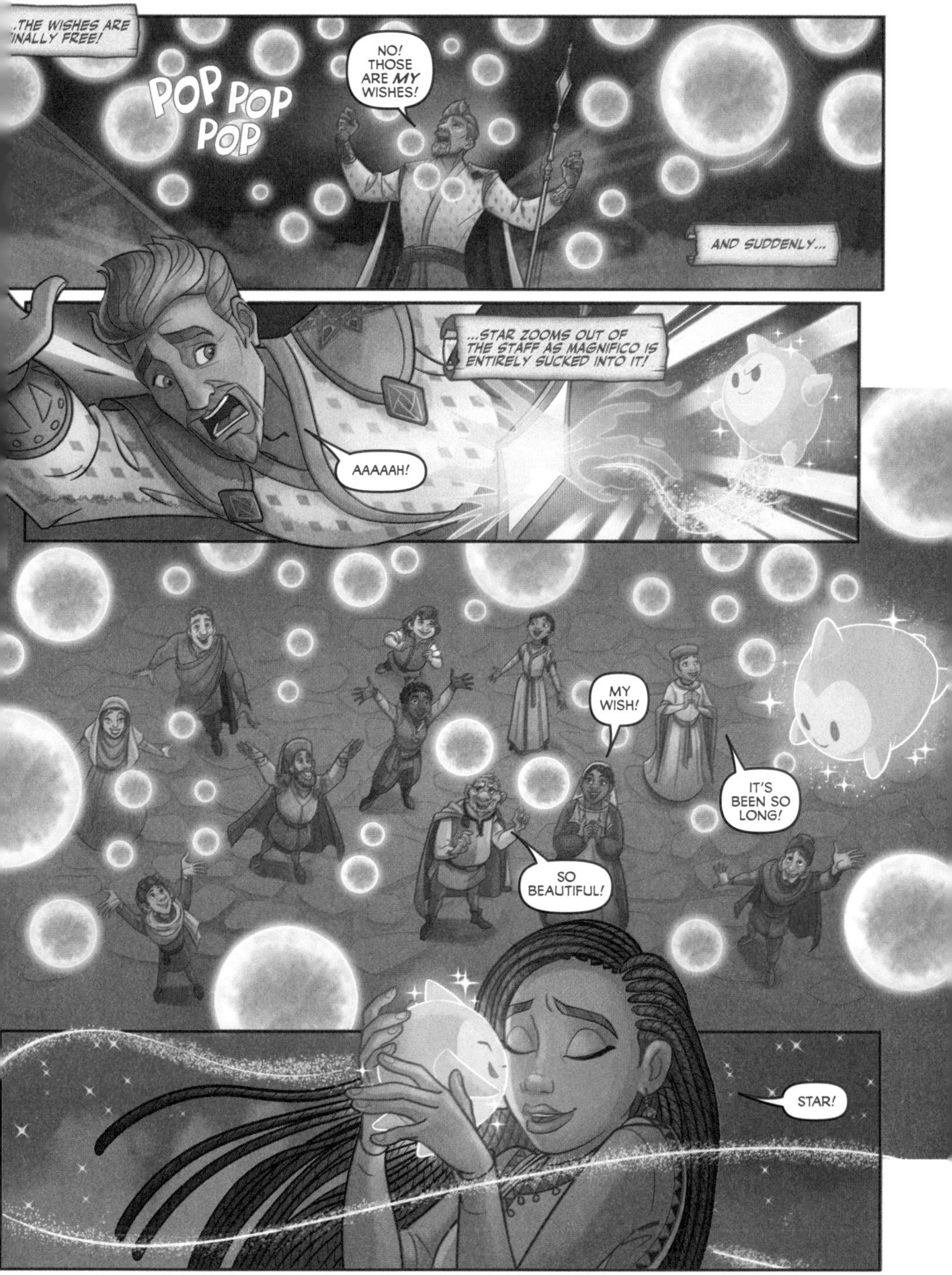
...THE WISHES ARE FINALLY FREE!
POP POP POP
NO! THOSE ARE MY WISHES!
AND SUDDENLY...
...STAR ZOOMS OUT OF THE STAFF AS MAGNIFICO IS ENTIRELY SUCKED INTO IT!
AAAAAH!
MY WISH!
IT'S BEEN SO LONG!
SO BEAUTIFUL!
STAR!

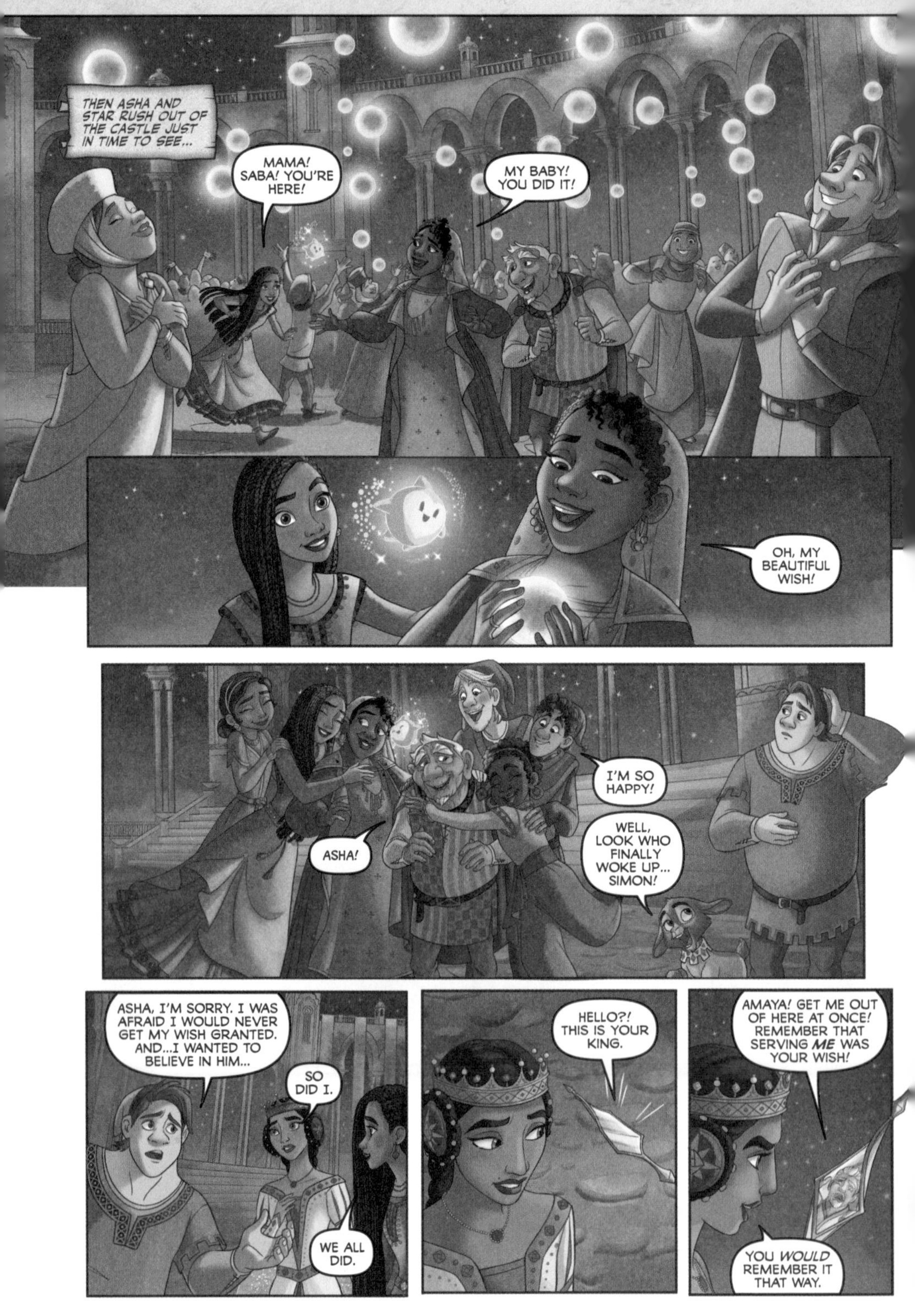
THEN ASHA AND STAR RUSH OUT OF THE CASTLE JUST IN TIME TO SEE...
MAMA! SABA! YOU'RE HERE!
MY BABY! YOU DID IT!
OH, MY BEAUTIFUL WISH!
I'M SO HAPPY!
ASHA!
WELL, LOOK WHO FINALLY WOKE UP... SIMON!
ASHA, I'M SORRY. I WAS AFRAID I WOULD NEVER GET MY WISH GRANTED. AND...I WANTED TO BELIEVE IN HIM...
SO DID I.
WE ALL DID.
HELLO?! THIS IS YOUR KING.
AMAYA! GET ME OUT OF HERE AT ONCE! REMEMBER THAT SERVING ME WAS YOUR WISH!
YOU WOULD REMEMBER IT THAT WAY.

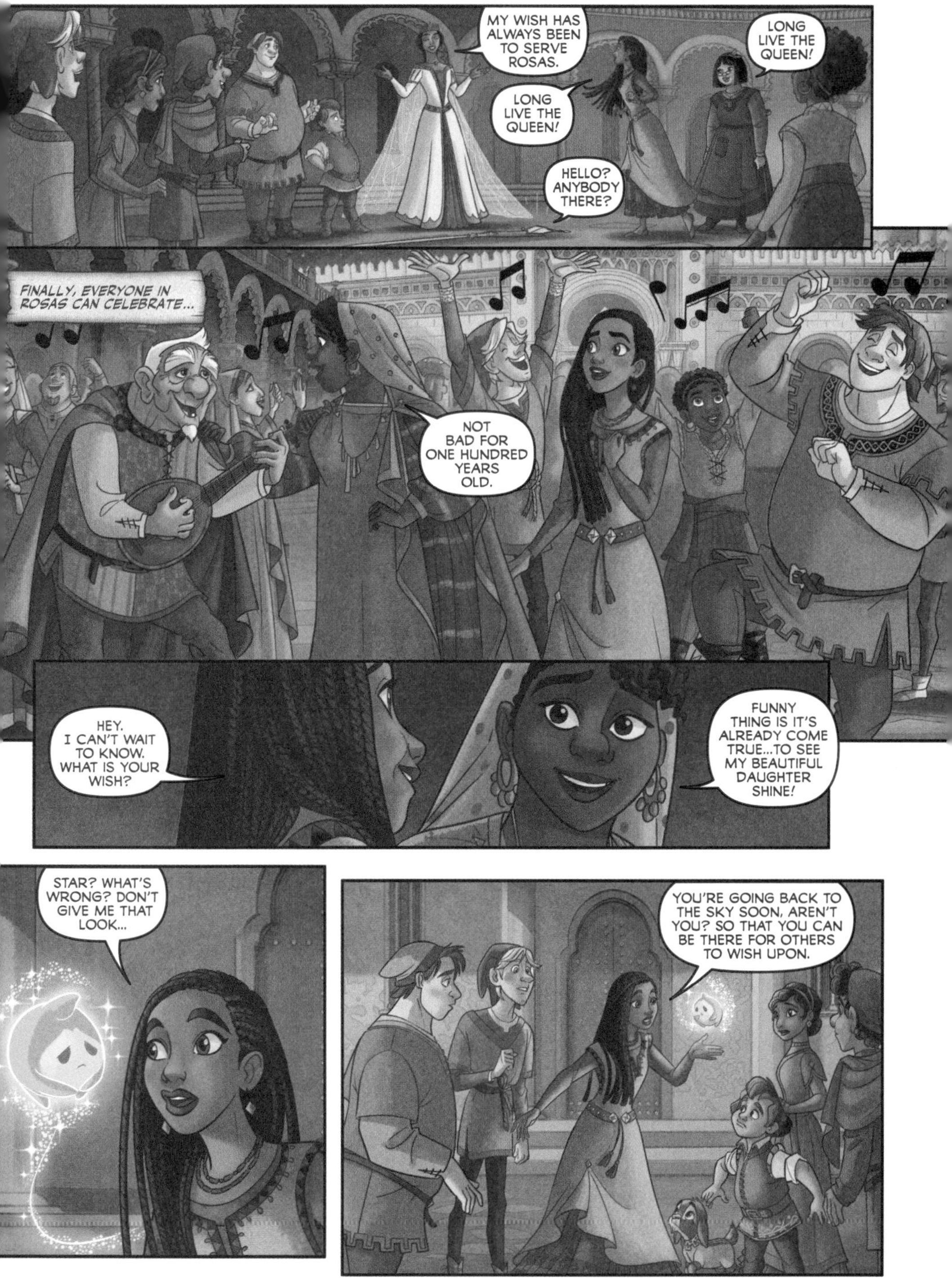
MY WISH HAS ALWAYS BEEN TO SERVE ROSAS.
LONG LIVE THE QUEEN!
LONG LIVE THE QUEEN!
HELLO? ANYBODY THERE?
FINALLY, EVERYONE IN ROSAS CAN CELEBRATE...
NOT BAD FOR ONE HUNDRED YEARS OLD.
HEY. I CAN'T WAIT TO KNOW. WHAT IS YOUR WISH?
FUNNY THING IS IT'S ALREADY COME TRUE...TO SEE MY BEAUTIFUL DAUGHTER SHINE!
STAR? WHAT'S WRONG? DON'T GIVE ME THAT LOOK...
YOU'RE GOING BACK TO THE SKY SOON, AREN'T YOU? SO THAT YOU CAN BE THERE FOR OTHERS TO WISH UPON.

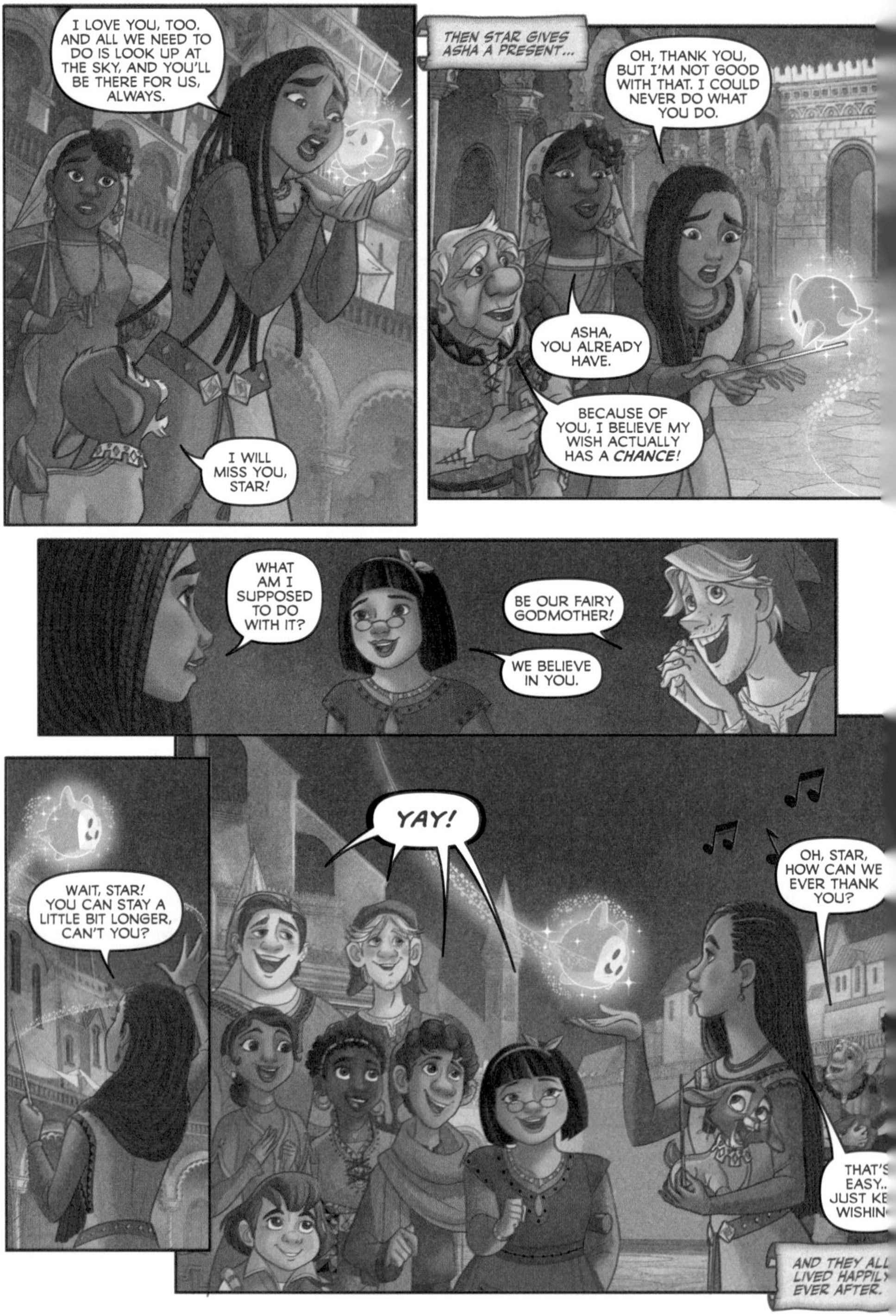
I LOVE YOU, TOO. AND ALL WE NEED TO DO IS LOOK UP AT THE SKY, AND YOU'LL BE THERE FOR US, ALWAYS.
I WILL MISS YOU, STAR!
THEN STAR GIVES ASHA A PRESENT...
OH, THANK YOU, BUT I'M NOT GOOD WITH THAT. I COULD NEVER DO WHAT YOU DO.
ASHA, YOU ALREADY HAVE.
BECAUSE OF YOU, I BELIEVE MY WISH ACTUALLY HAS A *CHANCE*!
WHAT AM I SUPPOSED TO DO WITH IT?
BE OUR FAIRY GODMOTHER!
WE BELIEVE IN YOU.
WAIT, STAR! YOU CAN STAY A LITTLE BIT LONGER, CAN'T YOU?
YAY!
OH, STAR, HOW CAN WE EVER THANK YOU?
THAT'S EASY.. JUST KE WISHIN
AND THEY ALL LIVED HAPPIL EVER AFTER.

SCRIPT ADAPTATION Tea Orsi
LAYOUT Emilio Urbano
INK Marco Forcelloni, Sara Storino

COLOR Massimo Rocca, Cristina Spagnoli, Maaw Illustration
LETTERING Chris Dickey **GRAPHIC DESIGN** Chris Dickey

COVER
LAYOUT Marco Ghiglione
INK Marco Forcelloni
COLOR Massimo Rocca